Doom Sword

The force flung him backwards as he arced the
sword through the air. . . . He heard a crack,
saw a flash of bright blue light, and the universe
seemed stunned.

For the briefest instant the storm seemed to
hold back and the creature in the hall faltered
as if unsure. Then, as it reached for the door,
Adam held up the sword and the room exploded. . . .

There was an empty moment when he drifted
through space like a stunned butterfly.

The world was a blue pearl gleaming on folds
of black. The stars were tiny sparks cast from
a raging fire. Time was just a step between one
world and the next.

Then there was darkness.

Also in the Point Fantasy series:

POINT FANTASY

DOOM SWORD

Peter Beere

Cover illustration by Mark Taylor

SCHOLASTIC

Scholastic Children's Books,
Scholastic Publications Ltd,
7–9 Pratt Street, London NW1 0AE, UK

Scholastic Inc.,
730 Broadway, New York, NY 10003, USA

Scholastic Canada Ltd,
123 Newkirk Road, Richmond Hill,
Ontario, Canada L4C 3G5

Ashton Scholastic Pty Ltd,
P O Box 579, Gosford, New South Wales,
Australia

Ashton Scholastic Ltd,
Private Bag 1, Penrose, Auckland,
New Zealand

First published by Scholastic Publications Ltd, 1993

Text copyright © Peter Beere, 1993
Cover illustration copyright © Mark Taylor, 1993

ISBN 0 590 55288 0

Typeset by TW Typesetting, Midsomer Norton, Avon
Printed by Cox & Wyman Ltd, Reading, Berks.

10 9 8 7 6 5 4 3 2 1

CONTENTS

PART 1

The Ancient Warrior

PROLOGUE

n the final days of the war with demons, men gained the Doom Sword. The blade was forged for a mighty warrior by wizards locked in caves hidden in lonely hills. The Doom Sword claimed the world, and brought down the demons, and passed the power to men. But with every victory there is a price to pay, and dark magic stole the sword from the ancient warrior. And with it went his soul, condemned for evermore to dwell in purgatory. . . .

For seven centuries the new kings were at war, seeking the Doom Sword. The sky was poisoned, and the seas flowed red with blood, and fathers killed their sóns in the quest to find the sword; for the Doom Sword possessed the power to transform men into gods, or bring down the heavens.

Fleeing the slaughter the old kings headed east, abandoning their home to the madness blazing there; and on his long journey, one of the ancient kings happened across the blade. It seemed by accident, and the old king, pure of heart, thought he could mend the sword and cleanse its poisoned heart. He sat for seven years in conflict with the blade, wrestling its twisted arts.

But the sword was evil, for its death-blessed spells ran deep, and the king was torn apart by a creature born in Hell. And the sword lay in a pit, concealed for four decades, until a youth saw it.

Knowing almost nothing of the threat the Doom Sword posed, the youth threw down a rope and climbed into the pit, and as he touched the blade the darkness leapt from it to lodge inside his soul. The youth aged quickly, becoming black and spent, condemned to roam the earth destroying all he passed, and all who touched his hand were sacrificed in flame as Hell's torments stalked his path. When the young kings heard of this they hastened to the land, and the youth was forced to flee to uncharted western hills, where fools who still believe that the youth resides there continue to offer up blood to him.

But while the young kings hunted, wasting their years and men, another traced the youth's trail back towards the pit, and there, beneath the dirt which breathes a stench like death, a dark knight found the sword. His name was Kalidor, and he came from the west; a cruel, despotic lord who rode with drunken hordes. His fleet once sailed the seas up to the ocean's end, feared and despised by all. In pursuit of the Doom Sword the knight had put ashore, and carved a bloody swathe across the southern lands. The battles his hordes fought were the most dire of all. Blood-rain dripped from the clouds.

Shaken and astonished by the threat this dark knight posed, the warlords forged a pact to wrest back the Doom Sword, and they hunted Kalidor through the Kingdom's wasted lands, back to the ocean. There, in awesome skirmishes whose blood stained every strand, they drove him up the shores towards the northern hills, and slew each force he sent, and cleansed his raving hordes from every stand they sought. One by one they cut down his warriors, as Kalidor himself slaughtered the rival kings, for he was filled with wrath, and held the Sword of Death, though he had not mastered it.

Their final conflict raged on the Bridge of Doom, where a span of blasted stone bestrode an unplumbed gorge. The last two warrior kings took on the Lord of Night, with their young sons at their sides. They were the mightiest of the Kingdom's warriors, and their swords could hew through rock or bring down a wild troll. The battle swung and swayed for more than sixteen days, into a bloodstained dawn. On that final morning, as the sun rose above the mountain tops, a wounded battle-lord took the sword from the Dark Lord's grip, and in an act of faith plunged from the blasted bridge into the void below. Then the kings bound Kalidor, and scattered all his men, and bore him to the west, to a forsaken isle, where he could brood alone in exile without end, and dream of glories lost.

But as the years passed, and observation dimmed, the Dark Lord gathered ghouls and wicked sorcerers, and in the deepest pits beneath his Tower of Pain, set them to work for him. They slaughtered innocents, and gathered up their brains, and heaped them on the fires which burned to their evil gods. And for two hundred years they massacred and prayed, tracking down the Doom Sword.

When at last they discovered it they sent a messenger to the tall, lonely tower where

Kalidor held court; and, dropping to his knees, the messenger advanced, cowering before his king. . . .

"My Lord, the sorcerers in their unholy pits have traced the Doom Sword. Even now they attempt to bring it back, for it was far removed from the Kingdom's rule. The dog who stole the blade has passed away, it seems. They watched his soul ascend."

The servant glanced up from his deeply hooded eyes, and the lamplight on his face made it a bloodless mask. Beneath his tattered cloak his neatly severed arms formed humps like sleeping cats. "My Lord—?"

"I heard you," said Kalidor from his throne, where he rose to his feet inside a swirl of night. His black cloak hissed like snakes across the cold stone floor. His eyes were burning pits. "This place the Doom Sword lies," he said. "The way you speak of it – it is not of this land?"

"No, I fear it is not, my Lord."

Kalidor grunted as he towered above his slave, like a pillar of night, dripping with lightless fire. "This place, this far-off land—"

"A murky netherworld."

"How far off does it lie?"

The slave fell silent, struggling to find the words to pass on gloomy news without arousing wrath. It was no easy task, so he just took a breath and spoke as best he could. "I am unsure, Lord," he said unhappily. "One of the sorcerers said it was a different world. They work with charts and orbs, toiling like men possessed to bring it back to you."

Kalidor stared at him, with his fingers absently tapping his dagger's hilt. "The ancient sorcerers have had two hundred years," the Dark Lord whispered.

The servant nodded. "Yes, that is true, my Lord. But then, the sorcerers – you have had many killed. Those who are still alive are very sick, my Lord, from eating poisoned rats."

"Offer them food, then," the Dark Lord grunted. "Offer them anything that will keep them alive. I am too close to let these minor obstacles thwart my ambition. I have been waiting for two long centuries. I have my ships of war in the forbidden ports. I have assembled hordes who can devour a world – and they are fidgeting." He reached down for the slave and raised him by the throat, bathing him with a breath which could shrivel leaves on trees. "Do these great sorcerers, who do protest so much, swear on their immortal souls that they will retrieve the sword?"

The servant kicked his legs as the breath died in his throat, and blood drained from his brain. "I do believe so, I think that's what they said, they will bring you the sword. I—" The servant gave a yelp as the Dark Lord slapped his face. "They wrestle even now to bring it back again."

"Then let the war commence."

"The war? Right now, my Lord?"

"Have I raised deafened slaves?"

The slave stopped struggling as the colour left his face. "Oh no, I hear, my Lord. I was just—"

"Hear some more." And the Dark Lord took his blade, and carved an extra ear upon the shocked man's face.

The slave hung limply as the knife sliced through his flesh, for to cry out or protest would bring only more pain. He watched the Dark Lord lick his lips as he bent to his task—

"This good news pleases me."

CҺAPTER 1

Far from the Kingdom, in Norfolk's grassy heart, a funeral was arranged. It was a quiet affair with few mourners, and the flowers beside the grave took very little space. They seemed slightly abashed that they stood out so much upon the mound of earth. It was a Wednesday, which meant the town was quiet, for all the shops were closed during the afternoon. There were few growling cars to interrupt the peace which gathered round the grave.

On the gravelled pathway which snaked up from the gates, beneath a stand of trees resplendent in new leaves, the deceased's family mourned, in attitudes of prayer, staring into the grave. They were grieving for an old man who had enjoyed a long and full life but had died suddenly and unexpectedly. They had been unable to tell him how much he'd meant to them, or say a final sad goodbye. He had died in his sleep, with a soft smile on his face, as if returning home . . .

The service over, the small group wound its way back to the waiting cars in the lane beyond the gate. Just one figure stayed behind, looking down on the grave where his grandfather lay. It was the first time that Adam had encountered death, and he sensed that he must say goodbye. But the word lodged in his throat and he walked away, his heels brushing the ground.

His old friend had left him without a single word, after spending a lifetime refusing to shut up. When a man had so much to say, how could it be possible that he was silent now? All the tales he once had told – litanies of mystery, and places far away – who would tell those stories now? What voice could fill the void he'd left behind?

Only Adam seemed to understand that those tales meant something. They weren't just stories, they were the old man's life, and all his life Adam had been listening to them. People said the old man and his grandson had a special bond, which was why Adam could understand when others merely laughed. The stories touched Adam and rooted in his heart, and after a time the old man would confide only in him. He said Adam was blessed – though some would call it cursed – and must guard himself. He said a flame protected him and he should not fear it, for it was of his heart.

And the more the old man spoke, the more Adam thought he could detect the flame. He never told anyone of the pale blue flickering which hovered near his face or brushed across his hands. Sometimes the flame swept off to touch his grandfather – and the old man smiled at it.

What was this flame, though, which no one else could see? Why did it burn so low upon the old man's grave? Why was it Adam's fate to pick up on these tales and start to dream of them?

He felt very lonely as he walked slowly towards the gate, thinking that a part of him was now for ever gone. The two had been so close. . . .

CHAPTER 2

It took a long time for Adam to accept that his grandfather was truly gone. Several weeks passed, yet he still thought of him, saw his sparkling face as if he were alive, heard his booming voice speaking of kings and wars and battles on dark plains. They were such vivid stories, yet Adam believed them, for the old man spoke his words with such intensity. Sometimes he thought he even saw the world the old man talked about. It was a world of mountains and canyons without end, of horses draped in black, of riders carved from gold. It was a home to gods and monsters of the night – a place of sorcery. Sometimes of an evening, poised on the edge of sleep, Adam saw distant hills drown in the smoke of war.

The old man had planted his dreams inside his offspring.

Adam pulled open the door to let the man inside his parents' rambling house. It was a sultry June day, and the man was sweating hard. His vest clung to his back and his face was a crimson mask. His massive, calloused hands clutched at a seaman's trunk, which had jammed in the doorway.

"Is this going upstairs?"

"Yes, with the other stuff."

"Isn't it just my luck that Billy-Joe's laid up? I tell you, one more of these and I'll be on my back. I'll be in there joining him."

Adam caught the door-handle as the door swung back, and wondered whether he should offer to help or step back out of the way. After a moment's doubt, he asked reluctantly, "Would you like a hand with that?"

"No, son," the man replied. "One crippled back will be enough for today," and with a mighty heave he propelled the awkward trunk through the tight doorway. "They don't make them like this any more, 'cause they killed off the blokes was meant to handle them." The man gazed unhappily at the staircase straight ahead:

a winding, narrow flight squeezed between bare walls. "The bloke who built this house must have been wafer thin. How d'you get up them stairs?"

"I go up sideways. I'll give you a hand with it—" Adam's strong hand reached down to grasp a leather strap.

"Mind you don't bust a gut. And don't you let this drop, or I'll be marmalade."

They heaved up the trunk and put it with the rest, a tidy pile of crates inside the spare bedroom. There were no gods at all, just the boxed life and times of Adam's grandfather. . . .

CHAPTER 3

The hot summer moved on, and Adam came to terms at last with his loss. He'd stopped expecting him to walk in through the door, stopped listening out for his rattling motorbike. (He'd never understood how someone so ancient could be let out on the roads.) Yet though the family seldom spoke of him, the pile of trunks and chests stood just as they'd been left, as if sorting them out would be a final farewell to the old man. The chests grew dusty and mice built nests in them, for there are always mice in such homes. Sometimes, in certain lights, or in the dead of night, the pile seemed fortress-like.

It was on a steamy afternoon that Adam went

inside the cluttered spare room. He wore grey jeans and a thin white cotton shirt, and his hair flopped on his face in an exhausted wave. His dark, expressive eyes lingered unhappily on the things his grandfather had left.

Though the room was shaded, the air was stifling and shadows sprawled lazily on the floor. The pictures on the walls showed scenes of lakes and hills, but seemed quite bored by them. An orange butterfly trapped inside the window was beating on the pane with dull monotony. Another, on the floor, had long ceased to fight, and now dreamed of other things. The room was peaceful, save for the butterfly, and but for its frantic wings there would have been no sound at all. Norfolk was half asleep. Adam's parents were away, visiting relatives.

After some desultory searching through the items in the trunks, Adam found a photograph – a faded sepia print of the old man sitting on a porch, which must have been taken years ago. How could his grandfather have been so old? The old man had once said he was immeasurable. What did he mean by that? No one could be so old. No one could walk the earth for, what, two hundred years? The old man had liked his jokes, but that was very strange even by his standards.

Surely he *was* joking? He must have been. Yet no one really knew the old man's history. No one knew where he came from or what his background was – only the jokes he told. The jokes were woven into exotic mysteries, tales of a mystic land where dragons once ruled, where men fought with gods, wizards cooked up spells, and wolves – what were wolves? Wolves were the sly spies of evil sorcerers, who ghosted through the world plotting dark revenge.

Adam had to shake himself before he drifted off into the old man's dreams. . . .

Upon a high tower on the Kingdom's western shore, sentries watched the approach of war. They saw thick smoke rise like storm clouds in the west, and the dull, ruby glow of forges in the dark. They saw pale jets of steam rise from where new weapons cooled in tanks like reservoirs.

Taking their spyglasses they observed the wheels of war, on fearsome battle-carts which could bestride a gorge. They heard the steady chant of sorcerers at work, preaching their poisoned thoughts.

On far-off city walls men shot down messenger birds which brought tidings of war to spies among their ranks. Then rumour turned to fact as the truth materialized – Kalidor had stirred.

As evening's shadows spread across the sweltering world, Adam unearthed the sword. It lay in a long trunk, wrapped up in rolls of cloth, inside a thin scabbard. It bore a polished hilt of jewel-embedded gold, and shone like silver blood. Its blade was thrumming as if life stirred within, and as Adam's hands reached out they were touched by silver sparks. He felt a rush inside as if his blood took fire, and demons brushed his brain.

Setting down the sword he stepped back a pace, pondering what dark designs must have confused his mind. If this was just a dream, born of the old man's tales, it was strangely electrifying. . . .

CHAPTER 4

"*My Lord, the sorcerers have raised a demon to liberate the sword.*"

The Dark Lord glanced up from his crumpled charts of war, and pushed aside a flask of wine which had been soured with blood.

"*This demon they have called, it will not succumb to the blade?*"

"*No, Lord, it is invincible . . .*"

A roll of thunder caused Adam to look up from his idle reverie. Night had descended with startling suddenness, falling across the world like a broad, black cloak. The dense air writhed and heaved as if caught in the flow of currents from the sky. In the dark window he saw his own pale face, reflecting back at him like an astonished ghost. The room behind his back blurred into pools of gloom through which strange whispers stirred.

Adam's body shuddered as he closed the curtains on a brooding storm which spread like hungry fire. A strong wind from the east bent flat the tall fir trees in the fields opposite.

A flash of lightning sparked through the boiling sky. The shadows of the room shrank back, then grew again. Called from its netherworld by dark sorcerers on the isle, a great beast had reached the earth. Its heart had been torn out, and the beast possessed no soul. Its cloak was midnight black, its eyes were blazing coals. It was a lord of Hell which scorched the very ground it set foot upon. . . .

Adam switched on a lamp to drive away the gloom, and listened to the storm. It would be some time yet before his parents returned, and with them absent the house seemed strangely tense, as if the rooms themselves could sense that this strange storm was nothing natural. It seemed too violent and rose up too quickly, and the very house itself was trapped right at its heart, as if a storm-cocoon had wrapped around the walls to shield them from the world.

Adam had lived through storms before, but

not the kind of storm in which strange voices moaned and lightning seemed to single out his house for attention. He could sense it crackling across the wind-blown thatch, plucking out clumps of reed to toss like shreds of rag. He could hear a savage gale pounding on the window panes as if intent on breaking the glass.

Then he saw the blue flame flickering above the chests and trunks – a dancing veil of light which seemed to pulse with life. A voice which seemed like that of a young woman spoke in his startled brain, saying, *"Pick up the Doom Sword."*

Pick up the Doom Sword. . . . He had heard the name before, had heard his grandfather speak of that deadly blade; a blade once forged for good which tasted evil ways and turned hungry for blood. He had heard that nations had gone to war for it and fought for centuries to turn it to their cause. He had heard that sorcerers gave up their lives in the quest to fathom its ways.

Yet surely they were stories and nothing more; no such blade could exist. But still the voice cried out, *"The beast from Hell has come. Pick up the Doom Sword.* . . ."

Adam felt strangely helpless as the storm displayed its force; he felt confused and lost and out of control. The strange voice panicked him, the blue flame startled him, he could not think clearly. . . .

Then, with a crash like thunder, the storm entered the house, flinging back the oak door and raging along the halls. The walls and ceilings cracked as lightning blazed ahead, clearing the black beast's trail. . . .

It was the lord of torment, which had not any soul: the blackened, withered husk of the Ancient Warrior. The creature summoned from Hell had now entered the house and was lumbering up the stairs. . . .

In total panic Adam tripped and hit the floor as the beast howled. The blue flame danced in his face, urging him to respond and pick up the Doom Sword. But he was frozen, and could only stand and watch as shadows filled the room and the startled lamp flickered. He was moments away from coming face to face with the rage of centuries.

Then he started moving, if only to chase away the flame which was driving him mad with its incessant prompting. The sword sprang to his hand, and its grip seemed to throb with a madness of its own. The blade thrummed as if possessed of life; white sparks burst from its tip to blaze across the floor, and Adam unleashed its rage.

The force flung him backwards as he arced the sword through the air, slicing it through chests and trunks as though they were not there. He heard a crack, saw a flash of bright blue light, and the universe seemed stunned.

For the briefest instant the storm seemed to hold back and the creature in the hall faltered as if unsure. Then, as it reached for the door, Adam held up the sword and the room exploded. . . .

There was an empty moment when he drifted through space like a stunned butterfly.

The world was a blue pearl gleaming on folds of black. The stars were tiny sparks cast from a raging fire. Time was just a step between one world and the next.

Then there was darkness.

CHAPTER 5

He woke up groaning on a bed of grass, beneath a blazing sun.

It was not Norfolk, he was fairly sure of that. Norfolk was not so hot, nor was the sun so bright. Norfolk did not boast clouds swirling round mountain peaks in the far distance.

Adam was in the Kingdom: the world of Kalidor, home to dark sorcery. But the only thing he knew was that he hurt like sin in every bone he had.

In the humid depths of a mighty forest which spread like tapestry across the southern lands, a pack of sleek grey wolves ghosted through the trees, intent on savagery. The beasts had travelled a long way from their cold northern home, seeking the warming blood of the wild forest herds. They had killed many deer on their path through the trees, yet still their bellies moaned.

With every year now the wolves spread their domain, expanding further south across the hills and plains right to the forest's heart which once had seemed impregnable. With them they brought a curse: a stench of dirt and gloom which would not fade away. Whole tracts of land lay waste when the wolf packs wandered on.

There are some parts of the forest you don't go to, no matter how sorely pressed.

The huntress forgot that in the tension of the chase, and strayed from her usual path. Lina had her crossbow and a dagger of thin steel. Her skin was smooth and brown, her eyes blue-grey. Her hair was tied back out of the way. She was seventeen years old.

Now she had her quarry boxed in by a stand of dense thorn trees, the deer having failed in its attempts to shake her off its trail. It seemed to understand that she had beaten it. She raised her bow, aimed the arrow's tip of polished steel at the deer's heart, and breathed one quick prayer. Then a grey tide swept down from the trees, and streamed across the glade towards the frightened hind. As Lina lowered her bow she saw the first wolf lunge to pull down its shocked prey.

In a blur of fury, the hind crashed to the ground. Hooves flashed through blood and she let out one brief scream. And then the beast was dead, and twelve or thirteen wolves were tearing her apart.

Lina's limbs stiffened as she watched this ballet of death. A chilling shade had crept through the trees and it seemed as if all life and hope had been sucked from the leaves. Her dark hair shimmered as she backed off through the trees, forcing through gripping thorns, stamping down stinging weeds. She caught the stench of death which drifted on the breeze. . . .

Then Lina turned and fled.

Shadows were lengthening as Adam bathed his face in water from a stream.

The breeze had shifted and now came from the west, bearing an acrid taste which spoiled the forest air. It was the reek of smoke carried from army camps strung out along the shores. The Kingdom's warriors were gathering in the west, taking up their rusted arms to confront Kalidor. The grey sky swirled with dust as armies on the plains marched to their destinies.

Adam was aware of none of this. His only concern was to find his way back home. It seemed fairly clear to him that he had slipped into a dream brought on by the storm. If he could just keep calm he had nothing to fear, except fear itself.

And he could sense a real fear as he glanced around the glade. The trees looked grim and bare as night crept across the ground. He sensed the stench of wolves. . . .

CHAPTER 6

A light was burning in the window of a shanty hut set some way from a path. Lofty trees arched across the roof as if consoling it, groaning as they shifted in a breeze. Their dark leaves whispered to a log pile underneath, which gave out no sound at all but may have been listening.

Beyond the log pile stood two horses, tethered to long thin ropes which wound back through the trees. A fire burned in a pit, breathing out clouds of smoke to keep stray wolves at bay.

Beyond the low fire there was nothing save the immense black trees which framed the scene. But for the cries of wolves on their distant forays, all was peaceful.

Shaken by his experiences, Adam did not think it wise to march straight to the door. Instead he hugged the trees, and skirted round the horses to check the window. If this was all a dream, as he believed it was, there was no way of knowing what he might dream up next.

He saw Lina bending across a smoking hearth, scraping meat into a pan. Her hair hung loose and swung around her face, and she wore a short brown smock. She must have sensed that Adam was staring at her legs, because she straightened suddenly.

"Is someone out there?"

Adam darted to the door and was about to knock when she swung it back. He had propped the sword against the wall, out of sight. Now he tried smiling hard. "I shouldn't be here—"

"So go away," she said, and slammed the door on him.

Some hours later Adam was sitting feeding the fire with leaves and twigs, when she came out to him. His hands and face were black from the shifting, clinging smoke and his eyes were red and sore.

Lina had tied back her hair and strapped on calfskin boots, which came up to her knees. This time Adam did not look as her legs came into view. He was too tired.

"I've brought some food." She knelt down in the grass to put down a flat tray.

Adam did not answer. He was poking at the fire with a long piece of wood which smouldered at its tip. He was wondering if this could be the longest anyone had ever dreamed.

"I said there's food there." Lina touched him on the arm and he smelt the musky perfumes in her hair. "Don't let it go to waste . . ."

The camp fire burned out as dawn crept through the trees to light up Adam's face. He was lying on his left side in the long dew-soaked grass, one hand beneath his face, his back turned to the hut. From time to time he twitched like a dog in a dream, and shadows crossed his face. He was having nightmares of the Ancient Warrior, the tortured fiend he saw as he plunged through the void. He was imagining it was pursuing him through space and time. . . .

As the sun's rays touched him, Adam opened his eyes and slowly looked around. The sight was confusing, and his aching limbs troubled him, but he knew at once that he was far from home. It was like a body blow to know that this was reality and he was trapped in it. He was as much a part of it as the horses in the trees, the dead fire at his back, the silent huntress watching him. What must she think as she studied his strange clothes and spiky hair?

"I'm not a sorcerer," he said, as though somehow this ought to mean something.

The huntress nodded. "That much is clear," she said.

"I don't know why I'm here."

"Neither do I," she said.

"I brought back the Doom Sword."

"You must be mad," she said. And then she stared at him. Adam wasn't joking – she could read it in his eyes. He really thought he'd brought the Doom Sword back again.

"The Doom Sword is long gone."

"I brought it back again."

Shivers ran through her soul. . . .

CHAPTER 7

Lina questioned Adam for some length about where he came from. She didn't seem too convinced by his explanation, although she was obviously shaken by the sight of the Doom Sword. What most unsettled her was his ignorance of what the sword signified. He seemed to know almost nothing of the Kingdom's history, and she tried to fill him in as though he were a child, all the time watching for any hint that he was merely toying with her. She was unimpressed by his talk of his own world, which she placed on a par with a sick man's ramblings, but she was horrified when he confessed that he had not heard of Kalidor.

"Not heard of Kalidor, the darkness in the world?"

"He doesn't get much press where I'm from," Adam said.

"But this is terrible. He is the greatest threat this world has ever known. If he takes the Doom Sword he will be invincible; he will destroy our lands and make the world his slave. Until eternity we will walk in the pain that Kalidor has planned for us. Darkness will serve him as he now serves the dark, and his armies and his fiends will rule for ever more. And now this is possible, for you have returned the sword."

"I couldn't help it," Adam said moodily. "It wasn't my idea, it just happened that way. Something came through the dark – there was this awful storm—"

"A Dark Lord storm," she said. "He reaches everywhere through his black arts and spells. Even beyond the void through which the Doom Sword fell."

"Do you think my grandfather—?"

"He must be the warrior who stole it from his hand."

"He's going to like me, then," said Adam gloomily, as he rose to his feet and paced around the fire. Lina had rekindled it to cook some breakfast. Rabbit-flesh hissed and sparked on a metal spit. "Why don't we bury it?"

"Why don't we raise a flag?" Lina said scornfully. "Every dark man and beast will be out seeking it. He'll know the sword is back – it's just a matter of time until he tracks it down. The Doom Sword calls out through the evil in its blade – it is a blazing spark to those who walk the dark. Why don't we save some time and send a note to him? *Why don't we bury it?*"

"So what do we do, then?" said Adam, suitably crushed by Lina's ill-disguised display of sarcasm.

"I don't know. If it was mine I would try destroying it. I would plunge it in the Fire."

"What, in this camp fire?"

"In the Eternal Fire," she said, "which burns within the hills beyond the Bridge of Doom. But I cannot take the sword, for it would claim my heart and sacrifice my soul."

"Oh, great! What about my soul?" protested Adam, who didn't like the way things were developing. He didn't like the way she kept on looking at him, as if assessing him.

Lina gave a slight shrug as she turned the roasting spit, and fed more herbs and moss into the smouldering flames. "Your soul is yours. I cannot influence you. You could just run away, or you could make towards the Fire and be a hero."

"Oh, sure, a hero." Adam snorted down his

nose and glanced away from Lina to stare into the fire. "What you mean is it's too late as far as I'm concerned, because I'm already doomed."

"Not necessarily," Lina said quietly. "If your grandfather kept the sword through all that span of years without it harming him, he must have worked on it to countermand the spells. Maybe he found out things that no one else had learned—"

But Adam had been struck by a new, sudden thought, and turned away from her.

"All of those stories . . ." he murmured absently. "He was preparing me in case this day should come. He knew that when he died they would track down the Doom Sword, and he had to warn someone. But why pick me? He could have picked my dad—"

"Maybe your father's ears were not open to hear. Maybe your father's heart was tuned to other things."

"There must be other ways . . ." Adam said softly, as his brooding eyes glanced up to watch the roiling air. Storm clouds had drifted in quickly from the west, spilling across the sky like a stain. The morning breeze had chilled and the tall, creaking trees rattled with dried-out leaves. "There must be other men who can control the sword. Give it to one of them, one of your warriors—"

"The nations took a vow two hundred years ago that none would touch the sword. It is too dangerous – it would turn them to its will and we would simply face another Kalidor. Besides, in such times as these no one knows who to trust. Dark spies are everywhere. The lords are meeting on the Council hill at this moment, and my parents have gone there to counsel with the rest. And of one thing I am sure: they would not want it known that the Doom Sword has been brought back."

Adam turned to face her. "Why you and me, though? Why not present the sword to two great warriors? We'd be no good in a fight—"

"Speak only for yourself," she murmured casually.

"Why you and me, though?" Adam persisted.

"I have considered it," Lina said gravely, as smoke writhed from the fire and curled into her face. "My father's family was with the warriors who took the Bridge of Doom during the final days of the Dark Lord conflict. They sided with the kings who took on Kalidor, and fashioned his disgrace. I think that somehow we are linked through our dead ancestors. I think it is our curse to carry on the fight that our forebears began."

Adam fell silent as he pondered her words. Perhaps they were just tools in a much greater plan. And what of the thin blue flame? He hadn't mentioned that because he'd said enough and, just as Lina said, who could he really trust? Nor had he made mention of the Ancient Warrior, who he hoped had vanished now. . . .

"Do you want some meat?" she asked.

He nodded distractedly and reached out for a chunk which burned into his hand.

"You should let it cool," she said.

"I will next time," he said, *"when I've less to think about. . . ."*

The storm clouds mounted and darkened half the sky above the forest. The wind was rising and whipping at the trees. It flattened out the fire and smoke skimmed the ground. The badly fashioned hut creaked like a sinking boat trapped in an ocean gale.

"Is it always like this?"

"Only since you came," she said. "He must know the sword is back and celebrates with rage." Lina was struggling to batten down a sheet of flapping cloth which roofed the hut's spare room. "We'll have to move on before it gets too late, for the wolves will be abroad as soon as darkness falls. And wolves serve Kalidor: they are his eyes and ears and nose," she said. "They will smell the Doom Sword as if it were dead meat. We have to put some ground between the wolves and us." She gave a savage grunt and nailed down the torn cloth. "So saddle up your horse."

"My horse?" Adam bleated. "We're going on a horse?"

"We have a horse each. Do you not ride a horse?"

"I did ten years ago, when I was just a kid."

"Then try remembering." She threw down a pack and it landed at his feet. "Pick out the things you need from what's inside the hut. Take all the food you can, for these are desperate times. We may grow hungry."

Adam bent to grab the canvas pack as Lina moved away to saddle up the greys. "How far will we be going?"

"As far as we can get," she murmured absently. "There is a problem, though, with carrying the sword, for if Kalidor tracks the blade he can work out our course. We need some shielding cloaks, such as the witches wear. We need my father's aunt, the witch called Helena, who knows about such things."

"Where will we find her?"

"Somewhere upon the plains to the north of the forest."

"*Somewhere?*"

"She moves around a lot. But she is generally found near the larger towns, where she performs magic tricks for foolish travellers, and milks them of their gold." Lina pulled tight a girth and packed a saddlebag. She strapped her long crossbow across the saddle flap and hung a smaller hunting bow, with its thin metal darts, from her braided belt.

While Adam was still struggling to get himself organized she unhitched her restless horse and sprang onto his back. She murmured soothing words as he bucked at the storm which rumbled in the west. Thick veils of murky rain were slowly moving east, and would be over them within the next few hours. She thought this was a sign that even grim Dark Lords are not infallible. With the rain to shield them and wash away their tracks the task of trailing them would be more difficult, and the creatures of the night would have their work cut out trying to read the signs.

"Are you ready?"

"Nearly," said Adam, as he rolled up the Doom Sword in a length of cloth. It might not mean too much, but he felt happier with the blade out of sight. It unsettled him to think that it was calling out and leading foes to him like a blazing flame. The sooner the Doom Sword was destroyed by the Eternal Fire, the happier he'd feel.

CHAPTER 8

They headed northwards, following a dusty trail which wound between the trees. The forest rolled out around them: canyons of green and grey, oceans of red and brown, flowers and seeds and thorns, fat bees and hopping bugs, bird songs and rustling. Squirrels cavorted amongst the lofty pines; grey possums set up home amongst the broad-leaved oaks. Sweet chestnuts brushed the ground; bindweeds climbed up and down, choking without a sound.

Across the forest litter stalked caps of fungi, multi-hued nibbled domes leaking out tonnes of spores. Honeydew rained down on teams of ants which combed the forest floor. There was a thick scent of flowers and the reek of rotting leaves, the musty scent of earth underlying everything. There were hints of beasts, foxes or deer perhaps, rising up from the glades.

The forest spread itself like a great cloak, and like a living thing meandered up and down. It never stayed the same, but rolled and reared and dipped through crags and plunging troughs. It cloaked a landscape of rivers and ravines; of towering granite peaks and monumental drops. Waterfalls died in foam as if the forest wept. Flowers were the forest's smile.

To cross the forest could take several weeks, and there were those within who had never stepped outside. The forest was their home; they knew nothing of the vast world beyond. They would live and die there, raise up their families there, and would never think to question where they stood. If nations went to war and politics was king, they were unmoved by it.

Between the settlements which stood beneath the trees, there roamed a band of man who preyed on others. They were the rogues and thieves and forest murderers. Men called them *reivers*. . . .

Adam reined in to wipe the sweat from his face, for the air was stifling. They were in an area of gullies and ravines, where mighty conifers rose up like towers. Waterfalls plunged and roared, sending up veils of spray, and fine droplets covered them. Clouds of mosquitoes zoomed through the humid air, as if delighting in the coming thunderstorms. But they were merely shades of the clouds which lumbered overhead on their long journey east.

Adam's horse, Alon, panted wearily. The path they were following was narrow and steep, and slick with moss, and there was a yawning gorge a few steps to the left. The flies about his face were driving him insane, and he was sick of them. He wanted to return to the peaceful woodland and find a place to rest far from the stinging flies. Adam could sympathize with that. It was no great shakes trudging along a trail, getting your backside bruised while being eaten alive. He stared glumly around to see how far they'd come and sensed a shadow move.

Something was emerging from a stand of close-set trees, some fifty metres off, below a hang of rock. Something on jet black steeds with thunder in its wake. It was the reivers. . . .

"Holy cow!" Adam shouted as he saw the band come streaming down the rock, spreading out like a fan to cut off all escape, devouring chunks of ground.

He could barely move in the saddle, stunned

by the speed with which they moved and chilled by the sounds they made. If Lina had not leant across to slap Alon's rump they would have flattened him. She was shouting, whipping on the horses, sending them across a glade, crashing through leaves and trees, skidding on sodden ground and swerving round the clumps of thorn in front of them.

The beasts went galloping straight through a swollen stream, kicking up veils of spray which shone like silver lace. They took on fallen logs with awe-inspiring ease, springing like bolting stags.

Adam struggled to stay on Alon's back, dodging the earth and stones kicked up by Lina's horse, Ramadeen. Branches slapped him in the face and the sound of his own voice screamed in his ears. Each time Alon slipped, and he slipped several times, Adam's heart skipped a beat. For the trailing hunters were closing in all the time, driving their black steeds ever onward. In their tattered rags of green and black they seemed to merge with the forest's gloom.

Sensing the difficulties that Adam was having, Lina swerved away from the track and took a softer path, hoping to gain some ground within the clinging gloom beneath the black conifers. The two greys thundered through the woods, crashing through brush and fir, so intent on the chase that they almost forgot the riders on their backs. Each raced to beat the horse ahead, to drive up to the front. Their tongues hung out, their lungs breathed fire. They felt invincible.

The ground grew steeper and more treacherous; the tall trees were thinning out, but beneath the brooding sky the beasts rode on and on, setting a desperate pace. Now they were on a broken plateau set in the forest's heart: a place of towering cliffs where grey-winged falcons soared, a place where rivers plunged into great waterfalls which pounded the earth.

But the reivers on their black steeds were gaining now with every lunging step, looming up on Alon, matching him stride for stride. Adam could feel their breath snorting right down his neck; he could taste their dirt and sweat. Shadows like grey doom closed in on either side of him, wild shapes of fur and rag, with angry blazing eyes. He felt the wind of steel as blades flashed by his face, and heard a wicked sigh.

But he could go no faster, for Alon had given all he had. His horse was snorting blood at the end of its brave, doomed attempt to be invincible. Visions of slaughter passed through its mind: pictures of pain and steel, and dark blood pouring out. Drumbeats inside its head were the thunder of its heart. It gave a great leap to thwart its coming doom and crashed onto its side in a jumble of limbs, fighting to save itself on a treacherous slope which led towards a foaming gorge.

But the horse was falling, toppling inexorably, cartwheeling down the slope towards the landscape's edge, while Adam, his foot caught in the reins, was hauled down after it.

Down they plunged towards the drop, where silver spray rose up like veils from the gorge. Sharp rocks stood all around like knives waiting to strike; waterfalls crashed and roared.

As Lina reined in to watch their desperate plight, they hurtled off the lip into the silver clouds, then disappeared like stones, plummeting through the spume to feed the booming foam. . . .

CHAPTER 9

Adam hurtled into a cauldron froth of rage and water. The horse came thundering down several metres off, throwing up towering plumes of surface scum and foam as the echoes of its fall merged with the roar and crash of thunder from the falls.

Water closed around the youth, and the roaring in his ears practically deafened him. The cold jerked the air out of his startled lungs as shock made his chest contract. He began to fight his way towards the surface foam, held back by the weight of the sword which was strapped across his back, but every time he reached the light he was sucked down again, transported by the flow.

Smooth black rocks mocked him as his fingers clawed for a grip. The towering cliffs above were sheer as polished glass. There were no trailing boughs, no outcrops reaching out for him to beach upon. As he was smashed repeatedly against the canyon walls he felt the strength drain from his freezing limbs and sensed the awful tug of the maelstrom taking hold of him. Exhausted and battered, Adam made a desperate lunge to clutch a ledge of stone above the water-line, but the current sucked him down beneath a waterfall, then spat him out again. The force ejected him into a cave-like backwater, a sullen pool of black lying beneath the falls, where the rage behind his back was as complete and dense as a sheet of solid steel. Utterly helpless, he could only listen to the thunderclaps of waves dashing against the rocks. His heart thumped like a mad machine inside his straining chest.

And when he was able to look around he could see no escape, other than through the pounding falls which would pulverize his bones. Unless the thin vein of light which shone through a rent in the cavern's wall actually led somewhere. . . .

Up on the craggy rocks above the foaming gorge, the leader of the reivers reined in his horse.

The wind whipped him, tugging at his tattered clothes and making his long black cloak flap like dejected wings. The horse on which he rode was stamping on the ground, snorting out plumes of breath. As the black beast shook itself, making its harness creak, the man leant to peer into the gorge, shielding his eyes against the gusting winds which swirled up out of it.

He could see the grey horse floundering against the flow, straining with every limb to reach the farther shore. But of the fallen youth there was no sign; the half-drowned horse seemed alone. Either the river had swallowed up the youth, or he had been borne away, though it seemed impossible that he could survive the fall – not through that angry foam, not through those fearsome rocks which reared like jagged teeth.

Yet the reiver did not move off, for he was puzzled and disturbed. Something about the youth was nagging in his brain . . . something about his clothes or the items he carried . . . something on his back. . . .

The reiver was not aware of it, but Kalidor's will had reached out to touch the minds of men. The Dark Lord's will had said, *"Bring the Doom Sword to me. . . ."* and the reiver's mind had heard.

He was almost oblivious to the party at his

back, the group of grim dark men on their impatient steeds who were staring at the rising trail along which their fleeing prey was urging her grey horse. The girl was getting away from them while their leader Robart stared upon a patch of foam which promised no reward. But they did not sense the force of the Dark Lord's probing will, which was making him its slave. . . .

CHAPTER 10

The air grew rank as Adam inched ahead, keeping close to a wall. The crack had led him into a world of caves, an underground labyrinth of former iron mines. The walls had been shored up by timbers as old as time, which had petrified to stone. Grey light leaked through shafts bored through the earth. Water dripped down the walls, ore-stained and red as blood. The bones of lost creatures, which had found no way out, were piled in forlorn heaps.

Cave rats skittered off like leaves as Adam stepped through the gloom, clutching the Doom Sword. He held it aimed ahead, fearful of what might lurk in this forsaken tomb. For he had heard voices muttering within the clinging dark: voices which schemed of death and probed the ways of pain. The voices were quite low, but hard as Adam tried, he could not shake them off. Sometimes the words pursued him, sometimes they lay ahead. As those who whispered moved, stepping on old, dried bones, they sounded inhuman. . . .

Lina reined in Ramadeen when she finally realized that she was no longer being chased. The reivers had halted above the cloud-filled gorge, and were quartering the ground, seeking a safe route downwards. From a kilometre away she could look down on them from comparative safety.

She was on a patch of high ground overlooking the gorge, and was able to let Ramadeen rest beside a gushing stream. From her high vantage point she could see half the world laid out before her. Mountain peaks rose in the north and east and rolling yellow plains spread out at their feet. She could see the silver threads of rivers on the plains, heading west to the sea.

Overshadowing all of this was the forest's sprawling bulk, which spilled across the land like a god's discarded cloak. Its valleys and bare scarps were ripples in the cloth; its rivers were the seams.

The day had brightened as the Dark Lord's threatened storm contorted in on itself like a collapsing balloon, and the only clouds which stirred were the long drifting skeins of birds out on the plains.

As a breeze tugged Lina's hair she lifted Ramadeen's rein and let him pick a course across the moss-strewn rocks. She aimed him down the scarp, hoping to find a trail to take them round the gorge.

Two hours later they crossed a narrow stone bridge above a crashing stream. They were some way to the north of the spot where Adam took his fall, and the river had been slowly curving until it crossed their path. Here it would not be impossible to clamber from the water. The banks had caved in and sloped to the race in gently shelving tiers on which young willows grew. Here Adam could have scrambled out, and – as if right on cue – Lina spotted his horse. Alon was grazing a patch of blue speed-well, his saddle off his back and trailing on the ground. He looked no worse for wear than if he'd spent a night inside a rainstorm.

But of his missing rider there was no sign, though Lina rode some way upstream calling out Adam's name. Bare echoes answered back from the black cliffs opposite, fading out like snuffed flames.

Lina gathered up Alon's rein and cantered up a rise, scanning to east and west for any hopeful sign, though it seemed a hopeless task to locate Adam now in the forest wilderness. She hoped to sense the sword, for the spells inside its heart let out a siren wail, and once or twice she'd felt that wailing in her heart, like a distant trembling.

But Lina was also aware of something malevolent waiting up ahead. Something dark and obscene, older than the hills themselves, lurked in the Doom Sword's path.

Like two great armies they were closing inexorably; the Doom Sword's ancient spells and the black shape's poisoned art. Standing on the ridge Lina could feel her heart chilling inside her breast. . . .

CHAPTER 11

"**Y**ou have come to kill me," said a creature in the darkness ahead of him. Adam could barely see the beast, though he could sense its awesome bulk and taste the reek of death which hovered over it. He could smell its rancid breath and feel its streams of waste lapping around its feet. He was aware that it was watching him from eyes that loved the dark, for the beast was of the night and had long shunned daylight. And now he could see that thick, iron chains bound it to a wall where it was in suppurating pools of slime.

"At last the Dark Lord Kalidor has sent a murderer to end my torment."

"I'm not a murderer," said Adam softly, though he held his sword ahead to keep the beast at bay.

"Then put away your sword, for I have no strength to fight. I am in misery. . . ."

The leader of the reivers grunted as something in the air disturbed his reverie. It was a snarling sound from somewhere to the south: the sound a dog might make when fighting for a bone, so far away and faint that it was barely possible to detect it in the wind. Yet Robart caught it and turned it in his mind, knowing instinctively that the distant sound was of a beast of power, and that a force of hate had entered the world.

The sound came from the very fringes of the forest to the south, where poisoned swamps marked the Kingdom's end. Something rose from the mire to drink the fetid air and cloak itself with veils of fire. It was the Ancient Warrior, hauled through rents in time to hunt the missing sword for the evil Kalidor, though the spells had over-reached, for the Ancient Warrior was to be kept from the earth.

The ancient sorcerers on their ungodly isle, who had toiled for lives and years to serve the Dark Lord's will, had summoned up a curse which they could not control, and which threatened the world. Only their master Kalidor, grown sick and proud and vain, thought he possessed the will to send back the dark force and he alone was not afraid.

"What are you listening to?" one of his men asked, as shadows passed across the scars on Robart's face.

"Something far to the south, seeking the same as us. A rival for the sword." Robart's gaze slid sideways to look across the gorge for, just as Lina had, he could detect the sword. It was advancing beneath the cliffs upon the northern shore, towards a deadly goal. . . .

"Abandon the search here. We'll travel to the east to find a route across."

Robart gazed once more to the south, where the Warrior was still some way off, though slowly heading north. He must locate the sword before this new force arrived, for he was chilled by it. It spoke of an evil such as he'd never known, greater than the brooding ancient power beneath the nearby hills.

It seemed on every side dark forces were being drawn towards the Doom Sword. . . .

Aware of none of this, Adam faced his own problems in the complex of mines beneath the black stone cliffs, where a great beast barred his way, and the ghouls which were its slaves had gathered at his back.

The beast could swallow him, Adam suddenly

realized as his straining eyes adjusted to the pools of gloom; it seemed to fill the mine, so awesome was its bulk, so bloated its limbs. It was like a great slug or pupa wreathed in grey, with fist-sized breathing holes which wheezed and dripped out phlegm. Its teeth trapped shreds of flesh which hung like tattered flags. Its odour was obscene.

Yet for all its monstrousness, and the cloaking smell of death, it had not threatened him nor made a forward move, trapped as it was by the chains which pinned it to the wall, and made it pitiful. It moaned desperately and writhed as if in pain, its putrid, yellow eyes rolling in its face. "You have come to murder me. Kalidor pities me," the beast kept whispering.

Adam was both bewildered and shaken by the beast. "I'm not from Kalidor, and I'm not a murderer."

"You come to torment me," the beast wailed piteously, though it had cunning eyes. "Please kill me suddenly, let death be a surprise, for I am sorrowful. For a millennium I have rotted in these chains, craving death to end my misery, for I was a man until I crossed Kalidor and he cast me in this pit. He sent evil sorcerers to work their spells on me until I was transformed. For eleven hundred years my life has ebbed away. Please end it gracefully."

"I'm not a murderer," Adam said uncomfortably, as he tried to still the trembling in his limbs. The sword was heavy and he wanted to put it down. He wanted to sit down and find some time to think. He had been through far too much for him to comprehend, and this beast was troubling him. He sensed its cunning and feared the way it looked, and yet for centuries it had been trapped in pain. Should he not pity it, knowing that Kalidor had brought it to this fate?

As if it caught this thought the beast spoke urgently: "I see the dread I cause you. If you have space for pity in your heart, then kill me suddenly. I was a man myself once – a father and a son – and would rather meet my death now than endure one more day. Another hour would be too much to bear – my heart cannot stand such pain. Release me, that I may rest in peace. Strike me through the heart. Friend, be merciful."

"I can't just kill you," said Adam. "It isn't in me."

The great beast nodded, as though it understood. "Compassion is so great that sometimes she is cruel. We cannot kill to save, and thus we let pain endure. Such is the way, it seems."

"Can't you break your chains?"

"They have been wrought with spells. Nothing can tear them loose."

"What about the Doom Sword?" Adam asked cautiously.

"The Doom Sword's blade could cut through chains of steel and spell. But the Doom Sword is no more. The Doom Sword was destroyed. The Doom Sword—"

"*I* have it."

There was a dumbstruck moment when nothing moved or breathed inside the dark mine shaft. Not the foul creature, which appeared mesmerized. Not the dark, creeping ghouls, which hushed their talk of death. Not Adam himself, who was struck by the thought that he should not have spoken. He was outnumbered and weak from his ordeals, and he was not trained to fight other than with his wits, which were a useless tool when your mouth opened up and blurted out secrets. . . .

"You truly are the lord of torment and unredeeming death," the grey beast whispered.

"I'm not a warrior and I'm not a lord," said Adam. "I just carry the sword, that's all my part in this. The sword must be destroyed—"

The grey beast bowed its head. "Amen to that," it said.

"I could cut loose your chains if you would let me pass. But if you make one wrong move, I'll strike you through the heart—"

The great beast heaved in air, then bowed

respectfully. "You have my word," it said. "I will be your servant."

"I don't want a servant," said Adam. "I'm just releasing you because you've suffered long enough." And he took a step back to give the sword some space, and swung it in an arc as if to test its weight. The blade thrummed in the dark and tiny yellow flames trickled along its length.

He saw another flame flickering in the air – the same blue flame he saw when the creature burst from Hell. But this time it was hanging back as if it felt afraid to come close to the blade.

He took a cautious step towards the panting beast and saw fire in its eyes, dancing like hungry tongues. Then the mine glowed with light.

But as Adam raised the sword aloft to strike down through the chains, the grey beast leapt and roared and thunder filled the air, and a pus-filled strand of flesh lashed out and gripped the blade, forcing it from his hand. He was sent staggering backwards by the force which left the beast. Never had Adam known such pain and rage before. It flashed inside his mind and tried to clutch his heart. It almost blinded him.

At once the blue flame swept down like an exploding hawk to skim across the beast, blazing into its face. Flesh sparked and fat sizzled, and the grey beast raised its hands to claw out its own eyes. It was in agony as the flame sped down its length, touching, searing the flesh, setting the shreds alight. The grey beast lashed and roared, but could not touch the flame which was tormenting it.

As it let the sword slip clattering to the floor, the dark shaft filled with light from bursts of orange flame. Adam picked up the blade and sprang at the beast to strike it through the heart. The blade flashed in his hand as if the sword at least knew where the danger lay, and before Adam could think he'd struck a mortal blow.

The beast's scream was hideous and lingered on and on, as if the creature would not die but scream for ever more. When its last note died out the mine shaft seemed to ring as if bells tolled in Hell.

And then there was silence, and the blue flame disappeared; and the grey beast turned to dust beneath a guttering fire. The dark ghouls disappeared as if scared by the light. Adam stood caked in slime. . . .

When he'd recovered he travelled northwards towards the mine entrance. The shaft had been boarded up to keep out travellers, but Adam kicked down the barrier and stepped out into the air, emerging on a low hillside bathed in the orange glow cast by the sinking sun. The workings behind him seemed bare and empty now, as silent as a grave, devoid of any life. The grim, deceitful beast had been released at last to torment other worlds.

Adam had tasted blood through his use of the Doom Sword, and he would soon realize that in this warring world nothing was left untouched by the presence of the blade, perhaps not even he himself. For it seemed that all things coveted and lusted after the sword, and while he carried it there would be little rest. Now even he had fallen victim to its wiles, which offered only death.

He felt haunted both outside and within, envied, despised and feared by all things in this land. He had already fallen victim to the sorcery of the sword, and while the blade survived their fates were intertwined. There would be no escape until he tossed the sword to the Eternal Fire. . . .

Lina found him resting within a stand of rocks, sheltering from the evening breeze. He glanced up warily, seeing the huntress framed by the orange rays of the departing sun. The breeze tugged at her hair and the horses at her back snorted restlessly.

Lina did not ask Adam what horrors he had seen, for she could sense the shock and pain which had taken hold of him. Silently, she grasped him by the hand and led him down the slope in search of a cleansing stream. . . .

CHAPTER 12

That night they made camp in a shelter formed by ancient conifers which had been uprooted by savage winter storms and dashed against a cliff. Some distance behind them, the band of reivers was trying to find their trail in the increasing gloom. Waiting ahead of them were the perils and delights of their journey northwards.

They lit a camp fire, and watched the smoke escape through boughs like tangled snakes in the dead trees above. They saw the stars appear, to glow like scattered pearls across a jet black sea.

Lina cooked a rabbit which she had brought

down with her bow. They drank from battered cups which she fetched from her pack. Then they made a bed of ferns and settled down on it, close by the crackling flames.

Shadows stroked them as they lay wrapped in thin blankets, their heads resting on their saddlebags. Night breezes whispered in the trees, easing them towards sleep.

Adam kept the Doom Sword by his side, afraid to let it from his sight. Ever since the brooding mines he had kept it close to him, conscious of all it meant. It was a symbol of terror and of hope; an icon for the damned; a torch to light a path. It had fallen to him, a stranger in this land, to forge its destiny. He could not trust this place, with its magic and desires, and must do the best he could with the few things he knew. One of the things that Adam knew was that there would be no peace while the Doom Sword survived.

Yet it was so beautiful that he wanted to gaze at it; wanted to slide it out from its covering of cloth. He wanted to sit quietly by the low flames holding it, feeling its weight in his hands.

The blade seemed to be whispering as it lay at his side, urging him to stretch out his hand and take it up. But he knew the spells locked deep inside its heart were trying to seduce his mind.

He forced himself to think of other things:

he thought of all his friends at home and the family left behind, and wondered how he would escape from this new world, should he survive the fight. For it would be a fight to get across this land, where every tree and stone seemed drawn towards the sword; where everyone he met would prove an obstacle, who craved only the blade.

He looked at Lina as she lay beside the fire, her dark eyes wide and lost in the soft, dancing light. How could the two of them pass through this fearsome land, carrying that deadly sword?

CHAPTER 13

They left the forest in the early afternoon three days later. The sun beat down from a clear cobalt sky, and the air was hot as steam and still as shuttered tombs as they rode through the scattered lines of shrubs which formed the forest's front-line troops in its endless battle with the plain. Directly ahead of them lay a sea of green and brown which lapped against the shores of mountains to the north, which with their sheer grey flanks seemed like a mighty wall built to contain the tide. Far to the east of them a second range appeared, and somewhere to the west lay a wide seething sea. But their route lay straight ahead, across the arid belt known as the Kamalargue.

They fed the horses before continuing, and asked a border guard about the nearest towns. The closest was two days' ride away, straight as the crow flies. It was called Paridoor, and was a seedy place, with gambling dens and bars its main pretence to fame, but Lina thought that this was the kind of place in which her great-aunt, the witch Helena, might be found, for the old lady liked seedy towns.

As they spurred the horses out onto the grassy plain they heard a distant cry from the Ancient Warrior. They did not know what it was, but both felt their hearts tremble at the sound. He was closing in on them at an ungodly pace, carving swathes through the trees as though they were but chaff, cutting down every beast which wandered in his way and slaughtering every man.

As evening's shadows crept slowly over the plain, they sought a resting place. They were growing weary and stiff with saddle sores, and the incessant heat and dust had worn them down. A bath and feather bed seemed the kinds of things they would sell their souls for.

The inn which presented itself was not an ideal choice, and more the kind of place where fleas would fight to take your bed, but it seemed like a fair exchange for the stony ground. Also the night air was cooling rapidly, gusting across the plain as if on wings of ice. It was the kind of night on which grey wolves might prowl, seeking out blood and flesh.

They led the horses to the stable block behind the inn, and saw them bedded down in straw heaving with rats, then made their weary way across the dusty yard towards the tavern's maw. It was a rough and wild place where people came to fight, and they stood outside the door for some time trying to decide if it was worth their time to go in, even for feather beds. But the landlord saw them and ushered them inside, wiping his greasy hands on his greasy smock, pouring them greasy drinks out of a greasy jug, offering them greasy food. He tried to take their packs but Adam clung to his and shoved it underneath a table out of sight. They were shown to a booth much like an earth closet beneath the tavern stairs.

There they watched the gambling, the drinking and the fighting, and chewed the greasy food a girl brought to them. No one bothered them other than to look them up and down, for the customers were too intent on finding their next fight, and the pair soon realized that this raucousness was what men came for. It was not the rare food or the fine, exquisite ales – it was the camaraderie of thumping their best friend. But though many blows were struck few caused much pain.

After a time the pair forgot their surroundings and remembered instead how tired they felt. They were shown up the stairs by a fat woman who shared the landlord's bed and made the greasy food. The room they were given was just big enough to swing a cat in, so long as the cat was small and was gripped by the ears, but the mattresses were soft and stuffed with fine goose down, and the plain white sheets were clean.

They latched the window against the cold night air, climbed inside the sheets and blew out the lantern, and drifted off to sleep to the strain of fighting. They were both so tired they never said goodnight. The last thing they heard was an enormous thud as someone fell downstairs. . . .

Early the next morning Adam and Lina were on their way again, straight after breakfast. The sun was still rising, and a thin grey veil of mist lingered across the plain. The distant mountain peaks appeared like brooding hulks, shipwrecked on ghostly shores. Scattered acacia trees were marooned travellers, their branches stretching out in forlorn, mute appeal. Hawks from the eastern hills floated on silent wings through the still morning air.

They took the dusty road which crossed the grasslands, and mingled with small bands of fellow travellers, mostly tinkers and merchants taking their produce north, who paid them little heed. But by the early afternoon lines of soldiers were on the road, heading down south to join battalions there, and huge weaponry such as mangonels and arbalests forced them from the soldiers' path, making them cut through the plain.

As the sun grew vicious in a cloudless sky, swarms of ecstatic ants rose in their nuptial dance, and clouds of whirring wings made them seek the higher ground of a gently shelving mound. From there they could search ahead for the city in the north, though there was naught to see but a shimmering heat haze. Glancing round, Lina saw shadows stir upon the southern plain. Something was moving at a steady loping pace, raising clouds of dust from the bone-dry, sun-baked earth. It was a little while before even her keen hunter's eyes could make out what it was. When at last she realized she let out a weary sigh, and pushed her matted hair from her eyes. "The reivers come," she said, "and they have wolves with them. They are following the sword. . . ."

CHAPTER 14

The reivers reined in, wiping the dirt and sweat from their tired faces. They had been riding for almost fifteen hours, through a freezing night and a strength-sapping day, and only Robart's will kept his men going. But even the leader, though touched by Kalidor's flame, was finding it a strain to keep on travelling. His mouth and throat were parched, his eyes red and sore, his pulse hammering. He kept on blinking, peering ahead to penetrate the haze that shimmered on the plain.

The twelve-strong pack of wolves that the Dark Lord had sent as guides were little help. They irritated Robart with their relentless urge to push on through the furnace of the Kama-largue air. They would never tire until the pads and flesh were ripped clean off their feet.

Robart took out a rag to wipe his streaming face, which was so hot it almost gave off steam. "We must be close," he said.

"We're nearly dead as well," a reiver muttered back. "The horses are exhausted, we can't keep pressing on."

"The horses will press on till I say they can stop."

"And when will that time be? When they are ripped apart by flocks of vulture-hawks? This is insanity—"

Robart knew it was so, but could not stifle his urge to capture the sword. If he held it he could rule the entire world. He could kill Kalidor and tear him from his mind. He could bring down the kings and have them kneel to him, praising his majesty. He would be master of half the universe, King of All the Lands, purveyor of life and death. His men would be his slaves, but the richest slaves the world had ever known.

"We ride down the two youths and spread them on the plains," he muttered savagely. Yet even as he spoke he felt a force behind him, which tore across the world like an unholy fire; a force so strong and black that he could not but fear the depths of its desire. It spoke of an evil far greater than Kalidor's, which had come from a world beyond the knowledge of men. And the shocked thought dawned on him as he sensed its wild advance, that it was *The Warrior*.

He glanced behind him as if to see its face; as if to test the rage which could destroy a world. As if to name the beast which had now joined the race to claim the Doom Sword.

"What are you looking at?" one of the reivers asked.

"Something upon our trail, which bears down on our backs. If we don't reach the youths a torment will arrive to devastate our souls."

Robart said no more, but spurred on his black horse, lashing it with his sword when it shied reluctantly. The tired horse took a breath it thought might be its last, and raced across the plain. . . .

Inside their lonely tower on the lonely rock, sorcerers sweated as they charted the awesome progress of the Ancient Warrior who had entered through the veil. Would they ever find a way to turn the rampant beast? It had killed hordes of men on its journey north, and every death seemed to increase its power. It was darker than the night, and covered the land with swathes of blood and slime.

In desperation they sent a messenger to speak with Kalidor in his unholy tower. They sent him on his knees across a bed of coals, as penance for his presumption.

"My Lord, the sorcerers, who have burned many souls, made me their messenger." The servant glanced up with pain-distorted eyes. "But it was not my choice and I have paid my price. My Lord, I have no skin left on my shins and knees. Ravens have pecked my eyes."

Kalidor took a deep breath and said, "Get on with it."

"The sorcerers are terrified of the great warrior."

"I'm the great warrior."

"The other warrior. The Ancient Warrior. They say he has carved a path through more than half the world, and has already destroyed several towns as well as all the settlements and forest farms and inns along his journey."

"Then they must stop him," the Dark Lord murmured.

"They cannot find a way. He breaks through all their spells. If he should reach the sword he will be invincible. That's what the sorcerers say."

At these words Kalidor reared up, and fury gripped his heart. The servant blanched and shrieked before his master's gaze. The Dark Lord picked him up and speared him to a hook which was fixed to the wall. "Find ways to shackle him, to bind him, to slow him down. Send spells to blind his eyes, until I have the Doom Sword. When I possess the sword of death *then I shall carve its very name upon the Warrior!''*

Kalidor swirled away as his servant tried to ease himself down from the metal hook which stabbed into his spine. It was no easy task being a slave of Kalidor, but few thought to complain. . . .

The black steeds thundered across the grassy plain, the grey wolves at their sides. Tense on the horses' backs the reivers spat and swore, and lashed the powerful flanks with blades of ringing steel. The horses' lungs were snorting fire and their tongues were like a storm raging across the air.

Beneath a hot sun their strides devoured the ground, until at last, far to the north, they saw the fleeing shapes of Adam and Lina spurring on their own exhausted steeds in search of Paridoor. Their flight seemed doomed, though, for the reivers were possessed. They bore pain and death in their unsheathed blades. They would run down the young pair and flood the plain with their blood. They would raise up palaces when Robart took the sword, for they would be his men, lords of his new domain. Their minds were filled with dreams and promises of gold. Then Armageddon came. . . .

It came like lightning descending on their backs, with a roar of death which drowned all other sounds. It came with dripping fire and poison in its blade, and brought eternity. As the Ancient Warrior exploded in their midst, he cut down six of them with one sweep of his hand. His sunken, bloodless eyes blazed with a ghastly light brought from the pits of Hell.

The reivers were obstacles between him and his prey and had to be removed. He swung round with his sword and struck one man clean through the heart. His horse, cloaked with fire, reared itself from the ground to paw the shell-shocked air. The swirling rags the Warrior wore seemed to blacken the day, as if night rode with him. . . .

On a low hill which climbed above the plain, Adam and Lina froze.

They could feel the Warrior wreaking havoc at their backs. They could hear the reivers' cries drifting across the plain. Looking back they saw a fine blood-haze spreading across the air and signs of slaughter on the ground. They saw the Ancient Warrior as a figure bathed in fire, slashing to right and left to cut down the reivers. They saw the blackened hole which had once held his heart, and they felt his gaze turn to them. Across the arid grass they saw his blazing eyes; saw him turn his black horse with its hooves of flame. And as their frightened hearts fluttered, the Warrior came for them.

His speed was staggering as he flashed across the plain, bringing his blood-red sword around to bear down on them. They heard his words of death, learned through the centuries, exploding round their ears.

CHAPTER 15

*B*ent over their black altars, the Dark Lord's sorcerers toiled to perfect their spells.

They called up elements from the forbidden hills, the souls of ice and fire, serpents which writhed through time. They strove to blend them all into unholy chains to bind the Warrior.

Then their servants flung the chains across the Kingdom's void, and shackled them to rods driven into the ground. They hammered home rivets, which had been dipped in pools of necromancy.

The whole world shuddered as the chains were fastened tight, and somewhere in the void the Ancient Warrior choked, for the chains coiled round his neck to jerk him from his horse and drag him to *the ground. As he fought back the links snapped in the air, and thunder rumbled out across the Kingdom's plain. And lightning sparked from wizards' spells, wrestling to hold the chain. . . .*

Adam's shocked heart leapt as the Warrior disappeared before his startled eyes.

He had felt utterly helpless as he watched the rider close in on him, knowing that he would die when his dark blade whistled down. He could not raise the Doom Sword to protect himself, for he was petrified. But as suddenly as the force appeared it swept away again, and a crackling in the air was all it left behind. The Ancient Warrior was dragged into the earth to do battle with the spells.

"Did you see that?" he said as the crackling disappeared, leaving an empty plain.

Lina shuddered. "It was the Ancient Warrior. He was banished from the world and lost his human form. His skull is all that remains, for the body he once wore took on demonic form."

"But I've seen him before," said Adam. "He was the one who forced me here. And I've sensed him in my dreams like a great brooding force."

"And now he's gone again, back to demonic haunts, as if tormenting us." Lina shivered despite the searing heat. "He may come back again, to force the sword from your hands. They say the lords he serves have even greater power than the evil Kalidor."

Their shocked eyes gazed back to where the reivers lay in spreading pools of blood on the blasted earth. Their steeds sprawled, broken and torn apart. Of the wolves there was no sign.

"Darkness warred with itself," Lina said softly. "And we in ignorance were best served by its aims. I think this is a sign that there is hope for us."

"Some hope!" Adam replied.

The huntress shook herself to loosen her limbs, and turned her horse around to face back to the north. "We must locate my great-aunt before the beast returns. She may fathom its mind."

They rode off slowly towards the far mountains, stunned at all that had transpired. Inside his trembling heart Adam was well aware that it was far from over.

PART 2

The Grey Witch

CHAPTER 16

The town of Paridoor crouched on the Kama-largue like a miasmal swamp. Its streets were humid and its smell atrocious. Smoke brooded over it in a dejected pall. Its windows were the eyes of creatures on black trees stripped of their branches. Above the rooftops hordes of black kites circled, and packs of lean grey dogs patrolled the crumbling walls. The gates had long since been removed from their hinges to serve as shanty huts. The roads which entered the town did so reluctantly, though travellers did not seem too perturbed. They came on foot and cart to lose their hard-earned cash inside Paridoor's bars.

It was approaching evening as Adam and Lina paused on a tree-capped hill to the south of the town, from where they could look down on the crowded streets and the camp fires in the squares. They heard the laughter of harlots in the bars and smelled the disgusting stench from stables seldom cleaned. They caught the sickly tang of slaughtered pigs and geese served up inside dark inns.

Tethering the horses inside a grove of trees, which were barely clinging on to what little life they had left, they hid their bags and packs inside a small hollow and covered them with stones. Adam kept the Doom Sword in its cloth upon his back, strapping it on tightly until it felt secure. Lina took apart her bow, but kept the darts to hand in case she had to fight.

"You'd better wait here," she told Adam as she loosened Alon's girth, "to keep the horses safe from any wandering wolves. It would also be unwise to take the Doom Sword down to the streets of Paridoor."

Adam nodded, and his eyes reflected the gloom which had filtered through the trees as the sun's light disappeared. "What about you?" he asked.

"I'll make my way down on foot and try to find her." Lina wrapped a thick cloak around her bare shoulders, and slipped a hunting knife inside her grey tunic. "I should not be gone too long – maybe two hours or so. Try to remain awake. If I find Helena she will want to move on fast, for she is not a woman prone to patient lingering. Be prepared to break camp as soon as we return, for we may ride through the night."

Adam hesitated for a moment, then helped her knot the cord which held her cloak in place. "Is this town safe?" he asked.

"As safe as any town where greed and gold gather." Lina glanced up with shaded blue-grey eyes, then touched his cheek with her finger-tips. "I'll be all right," she whispered. "Do not be concerned. Rest here and watch the beasts."

She slipped away from him and vanished in the night, blending with the rocks and trees. For a long time Adam paced, kicking at twigs and stones, awaiting her return.

Four hours later there was still no sign of Lina returning along the dusty road which led from Paridoor. Wrapped in a thin blanket, Adam peered down the slope, but could see nothing on the road save the lamps of travellers heading slowly northwards. There was no sound of foot-steps advancing up the mound, only the creaking of carts and clattering of horses down below. There were no whispered words, only the cries of men greeting their fellow men.

He was growing increasingly anxious, and the noises from the town, the murky, greasy smells, the flickering bright lights, served only to remind him how wild Paridoor was, and how alone he was. He could not remain there worrying about where Lina was, nor could he brave the town bearing the grim Doom Sword.

But loyalty is strong, and eventually Adam clambered down the slope to join the travellers. He tried to keep a low profile, but the Doom Sword on his back seemed to be crying out. He felt it like a flame proclaiming his presence, demanding to be heard. And some eyes turned to it, though it was wrapped in cloth, as though they felt a tug when the youth hurried by. They were bemused by him, this tall youth out at night, stooping under his bundle.

Adam entered Paridoor with a group of carts jostling to find some space. He faced a cobbled courtyard from which six wide roads branched, leading to cattle markets, taverns and bazaars. The roads were lit by lamps which glowed like great braziers atop high metal poles. A raging bonfire filled a pit within the square, where people stopped to buy pieces of roasted meat. Cages of ducks and hens were stacked against one wall a hundred metres long. Beggars were scavenging with a surly arrogance, demanding to be fed and objecting when they weren't. An entire chorus line of cripples and blind men took up one long low wall.

As a group of horses almost ran out of control, Adam picked out a road which looked less rough than most and, ducking from the lamps, made his way across the square, skirting the heaps of dirt. He kept his head down, but was halted several times when someone blocked his path or backed a horse his way. He felt so out of place that he could barely think more than a pace ahead. Alone and desperate he hurried down a lane which wound in cobbled curves through the dark heart of the town. Buildings and shadows loomed, churches showed padlocked doors, taverns spilled onto the street.

CHAPTER 17

After an age of searching Adam was completely lost in a dingy part of town. There were few street lamps, and even fewer people, and those who ventured out did not remain for long. They hurried down the lanes without a backward glance, their hands wrapped in their sleeves.

The sound of scurrying rats emerged from grim doorways, and the stench of food and filth hung like a brooding smog. The echoes of his heels died scared and lonely deaths in distant alleyways.

A scream of suffering came from an upstairs room, and a shadow rose to fill a window framed by rags. The plaintive mewling sound of a child which felt neglect lingered on the air. Adam crossed an empty square where gutters overflowed to send a stinking slime across the grey stone flags, and a pack of stalking cats shot off like ghosts at dawn, leaving dead rats behind.

A little way beyond the square loomed a dark passageway, which led to the nailed-up doors of an empty grain warehouse, and in the space before the doors he found a tense Lina, battling to protect herself. Three men had followed her, and finally cornered her in this lost part of town where no one answered cries. They were on the point of dragging her down when Adam gave a cry and sprang to her defence. He already had the Doom Sword unwrapped and in his hand, and its blade pulsed with light and issued howling sounds. He seemed to clutch a blade with a life all its own, whose hunger startled him. The sword was dragging him into a violent fray, and there was little he could do to try to hold it back. It throbbed within his hand, echoes ran through his brain, and Adam moved as one with it. He felt its power extending through his limbs, sensed the great depth of spells which were wrought in the blade. He knew no force on earth could withstand his assault, and he felt invincible. . . .

"Let her go," he said, "and go back where you came from, or I shall slaughter you."

The thugs were laughing, but without conviction, for the pulsing of the blade mystified them. One drew a long thin knife as a great flash of sparks leapt from the Doom Sword's tip. A tongue of white flame suddenly enveloped the man, cloaking him from head to toe in a blizzard of light. It lit up all the yard, and echoes of the fire glowed in the sky above.

A scream of terror mingled with the Doom Sword's cry – a howl of victory, a blaze of rage and lust – and Adam staggered back, fighting to hold the blade as it bucked in his hands. The blade was flickering with a pale blue inner fire. It was thrumming with the kind of awesome power which could destroy a land. And it reached into Adam's soul and pulled him down towards a desperate otherworld.

He fought against it, battling to gain control, trying to save himself from that awful yawning void. And as he fought the flames, so the blade bent to his will, till he half-mastered it. He had control of it as one controls a dog, and could unleash its force or send it to its rest, for the sword was in his heart as his soul was in it, and they found unity.

He stepped forward and the footpads dropped their knives and raised their fallen friend, who whimpered pitifully. They hauled him through the dirt into the alley's maw and darkness closed on their tracks. Only a silence and flickering remained as Adam took a breath, and let the Doom Sword's rage subside like cooling steam. He eased the tip earthwards until it touched the ground, and the last sparks drained from it.

When at last the sword lay silent and still in Adam's grip, Lina crept from the doorway she had sheltered in. For a long time she just stared, as if she felt afraid to approach the startled youth.

"You should not have revealed it," she whispered nervously, as she drew near Adam.

"I couldn't help it. It just jumped in my hand."

"Wrap it inside its cloth. We must depart this place."

"Did you locate your aunt?"

"No, but I heard someone say where to find her. . . ."

But finding the witch Helena, and actually talking to her, were two quite different things. When Adam and Lina tracked her down, she was bound securely and about to be consumed by a great wall of flame set in the central square. She had cheated rich merchants once too often, and was about to pay for it.

"This is the Grey Witch!" a man was crying out from the top of a cart which stood in the square. "The witch who is also known as She Who Cheats and Lies. Also, Helena." The man turned to look at her: a ruddy, portly soul, looking down on a crone who weighed a mere ninety pounds. Her cold eyes stared at him vacantly.

"It was I who captured her," the man cried to the crowd, which had gathered in force to watch the coming fire. "And thus, as law decrees, it falls on me to send her to eternity!"

The grey witch gave a yawn, and rolled her weary eyes at so much tedium.

"What about the Marshal?" cried someone in the crowd.

"The Marshal has concurred that this is fair and just. This woman stole a pig and turned it into a cow, which then gave birth to twins. Each of those accursed twins gave birth to other twins, and each of those gave birth to twins which fathered twins. And when the twins of twins mated with other twins, there were ten thousand twins."

"How long did this take?"

"About a dozen years."

"That isn't possible."

"It is if you're a witch."

"But where's the harm in it?"

"Because I bought the herd, and they turned back to pigs."

"You should have sold them!"

"Who wants ten thousand pigs?" There was a hearty roar of laughter from the crowd. "Besides, the pigs were cursed and no good for their meat. The witch brought evil to the pigs."

At this a murmur of disapproval rose, and every watching face turned to condemn the witch.

"So unless someone can find a word in her defence, the crone goes to the flames."

At the very rear of the crowd Adam and Lina were striving to force a path between the tight bodies. Lina's voice split the air as a winch hauled up the grey witch and swung her over the flames. "I want to buy her!"

"What? Buy yourself a witch?" The flushing fat man laughed, while the main crowd whooped and jeered. "What would you do with her, even if the witch agreed to be bound as your slave? And how would you pay for her? Do you know how much a witch is worth?"

"I'll give you twenty crowns."

"Oh, please, don't waste my time."

"I'll buy the witch with this," said Adam, drawing out the Doom Sword almost casually.

There was a murmur of apprehension within

the watching crowd, and the fat man's face turned pale as he backed across the cart.

"Just let the witch go free and no one will be hurt," Adam said quietly.

"Now, you just wait a minute—" said the fat man on the cart, as Adam gave a bound which took him to his side.

"Just let the witch go free."

The fat man watched the blade pulsing in Adam's hand. "Do you know what that is?" he asked.

"It is a sword of power, known as the Doom Sword."

"Oh, gods preserve us all!" sighed the witch. "The boy's an idiot."

"It is the Doom Sword!" said a voice within the crowd, and the name was like a fire spreading throughout the throng.

"But can you use it?" the fat man's voice whispered.

"I can cut you limb from limb and stitch you back again," Adam spoke.

The fat man's knees trembled as he saw the youth's eyes glow with an inner fire. He could sense the pulsing of the Doom Sword echo in Adam's brain, and the strength and rage which bound their warring wills. Leaping down from the cart, he cried, *"Cut down the witch!"* and vanished in the crowd.

There was commotion as the throng tried to disperse, spilling through the narrow lanes, calling the Doom Sword's name. The grey witch on the winch looked down with patent scorn.

"You made a mess of that!" she said.

They left the city as quickly as they could, fleeing like hunted thieves. The witch made cantrips to cover up their trail, and caused a cloaking mist to pour down from the walls, but she knew inside her heart that these were minor spells against the Doom Sword's art. It would be calling out to every friend and foe, urging them to its cause, trying to recruit their will. She could tell from Adam's face, and the tension writhing there, that he was wrestling to combat it.

"If you struggle too hard it will defeat your soul once and for ever more," she told Adam.

Adam did not answer, for he was looking through a haze into a lake of pain which was the Doom Sword's home; it was the secret pool in which the old mages had cooled the ancient blade. He could see scared lost souls patrolling on its shores, the victims of the blade which it would not release. The souls cried out in vain for someone to end their misery.

"You should not dwell there," the witch panted at his side, "for it will draw you in. The

Doom Sword is much more than a weapon, it is deep sorcery."

Her thin hands gripped Adam's arm as if to give him strength, forcing her own strong will to flow in his veins. But the shock was too much and Adam fell to the ground.

CHAPTER 18

"You are a brave youth, but you under-estimate the powers that are locked within the blade. You think you can combat it, and learn to harness it, but it will corrode your mind. It will turn you to a shell, and you will roam this earth like the Ancient Warrior." The grey witch watched Adam as he recovered by a fire, shielded from prying eyes by enchant-ments she had raised up. "This is neither good nor ill, for there are greater powers beyond the grim Doom Sword."

"I've seen the Warrior."

"I know," the witch replied. "They brought him to the world with their misguided spells.

Darkness accepts no bounds, and greater sorcerers than Kalidor's have died." She fed the firelight as Adam watched her eyes, dark and wise with the depths of time.

She broke up some meat and scorched it in the flames, then held it to her lips as if to taste the fire. "The Eternal Fire, whose warmth fills all of us, will be the Dark Lord's aim. To put out this flame will be his greatest urge: to send out dark despair across the entire world until his shadows spread through the whole universe and all men know his name." Almost unconsciously Helena reached into the flames and clutched a glowing coal. "He would crush out the world with all its light and warmth, and thus destroy us all."

Lina spoke from the shade. "We need some shielding cloaks if we're to battle him."

Helena nodded. "But they take time to make, and even then you cannot take on Kalidor, for he is both strong and weak, which is the Kingdom's curse, and confounds all of us. Kalidor's awesome strength would half-control the sword, but he would fall to its will as it controlled his thoughts, and that would shed a force which would kill all of us, whether he so desired or not. You must take the weapon and plunge it in the flame." She was watching Adam as if this was his fate, for no one in this land could hope to hold the sword. Her eyes were keen and dark, framed by her hair which fell like a grey waterfall. "You cannot fight him and so you must outrun him. You need us for guides as you are a stranger here. We must fly like the wind, for every ear will hear the tales from Paridoor."

"Then what are we waiting for?" said Adam.

The grey witch gave a sigh. "Because I cannot go yet. I have other tasks that I must perform first." She looked away from him, with shadows in her eyes. "We must deflect the Lord as he did the Warrior, for if we do not slow him down he will stride through this world and take the Doom Sword. My seven sisters, who ride on eagles' wings, say he now moves to act, and it is time for war. We have to slow him down and send out our curses. The sisters gather now."

The witch rose suddenly and turned to watch Lina, who stood within the trees. "I shall take Adam with me, while you ride to the north on the grey horse Ramadeen. Ride straight to Drabnaroth, the hamlet by the swamp, and seek the lowly man who is called Pignikker."

"He is called Pignikker?"

"He was a cattle thief. I can't explain it now. Tell him that Helena comes, and we will need a boat to take us through the swamps towards the northern hills. Tell him to stock it well and find us a mountain guide who can be relied upon."

"Can I go with her?" said Adam.

"No, I want you by my side. I need the sword near me. Do not question it." Then Helena was pushing the huntress towards her waiting horse, shoving her on his back with whispered prayers and rhymes. "He will fly like the wind and never swerve or drop. So ride! Begone, my child!"

And Lina was racing across the open plain before Adam could make a move to offer his goodbyes. He watched her disappear inside a cloud of dust.

"We must ride ourselves, Adam."

By the following mid-morning they were six leagues away from the town of Paridoor, with the Doom Sword wrapped up in swathes of cloth, harnessed to Adam's back. They were travelling eastwards across the rising plain, heading towards low hills which rose like dinosaurs. An angry sun sucked the last dregs of life from grasses close to dust.

As they rode through the grass, large flocks of birds arose, spiralling in the air like storm-tossed autumn leaves. Desert-hares crossed the ground with startled, bounding strides. Flowers, starved of moisture, died. Black clouds were gathering above the hills ahead, but they were sliding north, not troubling the plain. Low peals of thunder roared like gods beyond the clouds, tired from their weary days.

Adam was silent as he watched Helena ride on an unhappy ass laden with creels and packs. Her hair was tied in braids, which glowed in the sun like woven cones of steel. Her skin was as tanned and taut as a piece of dried-out hide, and her long-fingered hands were thin as birch switches. Her voice was strong and deep, and whispered to itself almost incessantly.

"I always thought that one day one of you would come," she murmured quietly. "Just as, for all the years that he was gone away, I knew that he still lived."

"Who?" enquired Adam.

"Your noble grandfather. The one I can see when I look in your eyes. He was a mighty man whose blood flows through your veins—"

"You knew my grandfather?"

Helena nodded. "I was once in love with him. He fathered my first child, who was lost at birth. Then grief took hold of him. It often crossed my mind that it might have been the grief which made him clutch the sword and leap into the void. It puts my heart at peace to know that he survived, and his line lingers on."

"But that isn't possible," said Adam, puzzled.

"The battle on the bridge was two hundred years ago—"

"We come from different worlds. Two hundred years is just a lifetime here. He *was* your grandfather—" Helena leaned backwards to tap the donkey's rump, and it made half a move to quicken up its pace. But when no more blows came it settled down again, and continued mournfully.

"He was a truly fine man. A noble warrior, who rode with Melindorm, who was our finest king. He could have been a prince, but he fell in love with me and gave up everything." She turned back to look at Adam, squinting against the sun, and gave what might have been a half-ironic smile. "So fall in love with queens, and do not set your sights on hell-cat sorcerers."

Turning ahead once more she lashed the stubborn ass, and with a shuddering groan it broke into a trot. Adam heard her witch's laugh come drifting on the air, and made haste to catch up with her.

That night they made camp inside a ring of rocks which stood like sentinels. The stars were radiant in the black sky overhead, and a half-moon glimmered down with a silver, lambent light. The air within the stones was as cool and ghostly grey as frozen fairies' breath. Helena made a small fire of grass and scattered bark, then dampened down the blaze until the embers glowed. Once more she roasted meat, and made a pungent stew inside a copper bowl. She let down her hair as she supped, and it formed glaciers unfolding round her face. It framed her deep-set eyes, and the shadows on her cheeks were like the wings of birds.

"I had another child," she murmured round the bowl, as if continuing their earlier conversation. "She was almost your age when she died on the bridge, battling Kalidor. She was the first one to strike a blow at him, for even in her youth she was a warrior. When the Dark Lord slashed her face she struck him in the chest, summoning her dying breath. You may have seen her . . ." The witch reached for her pack, and took out a lantern in which a blue flame glowed. As she set it on the ground she stared into Adam's eyes. "This is my daughter's soul, which searched the universe seeking your grandfather. She did it for the sword, and for the sake of the world, and to please me," she said.

A silence far deeper than the stillness of the night settled over the ring of stones.

Adam was awestruck as he gazed into the flame, for he had seen its light before, in this world and his own.

"When Raina learned of you she tried to protect you and guide you on your path."

Adam seemed mesmerized. "She is so beautiful."

"Such is the gift bestowed on those taken so young. Do not watch her too long or you will fall in love, and that is not allowed."

As Adam picked up the lamp and brought it to his face, he felt tendrils of warmth stretching down to his soul, and he saw a flickering shape inside the dancing flame, stretching her arms to him. The girl was slender, dark eyed and sensual. She whispered in his heart with words that no one else could hear. She told how sad she'd been, how lonely life could be, how much she needed him.

The witch felt wretched as she watched, for conversing of the souls was not permitted. The gods Helena served would take a toll from her for joining these two worlds. She was defying them to ease her daughter's pain, the pain of being alone for twenty long decades. The price the witch would pay might be her own sad soul, lost for eternity.

"My daughter, Raina," she whispered to the night, cursing her own weakness in capturing the soul. For the thought of being alone had been too much to bear, and she was damned by it.

*   *   *

The following morning they were both silent, brooding on what they knew.

The witch was impatient for them to gain some ground, and regretted her impulsiveness in showing Adam the flame, yet knew inside her heart that it was not her will that had commanded it. It was Raina, trapped for two hundred years, seeing only her mother's world, with no life of her own. It was her daughter's will which had said, *"I need a friend. Let me converse with him."* And now they had been distracted from the task which lay ahead, as though the Dark Lord himself had caused all this to pass; as though dark Kalidor, sensing where hearts are weak, had long since planned for it.

"We must move quickly," the witch said, shaking herself, "if we are to have a hope of besting Kalidor. You must put this behind, and save your thoughts of love for calmer, better times."

She spurred on her donkey while Adam trailed behind, dwelling on the flame which housed Raina's soul: a flame which he had seen take on the Warrior, and the beast within the mines. Raina had tried to help him, though she was but a tiny flame, and had tried to take his part against his fears and foes. Her flame had talked to him in ways no one else had ever talked before. She was enchanting him with her melodic words, and hypnotizing him with her elusive form. A dancing phantasm was wrapping round his heart, and lodging in his soul.

As the grey witch looked back a shadow touched her heart, and she felt the pain and grief which filled her only child. Maybe she had been wrong in binding Raina's fire; perhaps she should have died. . . .

"We'll never get there the way you ride!" she cried, to cover up the guilt and grief she bore inside, for she could turn lead to gold and transport fire through ice, but was unable to help her child.

Called from his reverie, Adam spurred on his horse, galloping through the dirt to reach the witch's side. But each rode as if alone, trapped with their secret thoughts, cursed by their own desires.

CHAPTER 19

The seven sisters of the witch Helena met in a secret grove. They met at midnight, answering Helena's call, and brought their flames with them to feed the constant fire. They set it in a pit which they dug in the ground and lined with flakes of gold.

"They're mostly senile," the witch Helena warned, as she and Adam tied their steeds to trees within the grove. "Don't let them read your palms or look behind your ears, or they'll find all kinds of things."

She threw on a cloak, a length of silver cloth which buckled at the throat with a still-living worm. She set flowers in her hair and made them turn to brass to form a burnished helm.

"Just keep your head down and keep the sword hidden, or one of them is sure to cut herself with it. And all we need is blood mixing with the spells. . . ."

Adam obeyed her words. He found a resting place beneath the swaying trees, and lay down in the dark cradling Raina's flame. With little sleep last night, he was finding it hard to keep himself awake. In fact, he was drifting away into a dream even as the sisters of the convocation formed their witches' ring. It was as though the enchantresses raised spells of secrecy, to keep their rites hidden.

The ships of Kalidor sailed on a midnight tide to form their fleet at sea. They were cloaked in a black fog which swallowed up all light. They carried footsoldiers and carriages of war. They bore the battlecarts, dragons and basilisks, lances and arbalests. Upon their broad decks they brought ten thousand steeds, each one a snorting beast caparisoned in black. Slaves rowed them through the straits and, on the open sea, unfurled the jet-black sails.

Along the Kingdom's coastline defences were prepared as the warships of the fleet rendezvoused in the Despotic Sea. The beating of the drums rolled out across the tide like the world's death knell.

While the alliance armies of the waiting Kingdom

formed their defensive ranks above the cliffs and shores, eight old and frail women met to concoct a spell to confound them all. They raised a hurricane from deep inside the earth, a twisting spire of smoke which swallowed up the sky; and with their ancient wands they cast it to the north, then swung it back again.

Growing and accelerating, the storm swept down the coast, forming a ball of rage which nothing could resist. It drew in winds and tide until it was a force which was unstoppable. And though the Dark Lord had sorcerers on his ships, they were taken aback by the storm's ferocity. As they worked at counter-spells, the black fleet of their Lord was sucked into the storm. . . .

"Wake up, Adam!" murmured Helena. "The rite is over now."

She took the lamp from him and stowed it in her pack as he rubbed at his eyes and sat up groggily. When he looked around the grove there was nothing to see; the witches were long gone.

"Did the meeting work?" he asked.

"I don't know. We shall see. We'll hear the Dark Lord's rage if he has been denied. But history will record that the witches gave of their best in the battle for the world."

Helena brushed Adam's cheeks with a damp

piece of cloth, for the air grew hot and dry close to such sorcery. Her face looked tired and grey; it was no easy task taking on Kalidor.

CHAPTER 20

Upon the sweltering plain to the south of Paridoor a bloody figure stirred. It had lain twisted and torn for several days, its mind lost in the fog known as oblivion. It had been baked and parched until its skin was raw and its tongue shrivelled to hide. It had been a prince, once: the reiver, *Robart Guy*, who with his band of men had milked the forest dry. But he did not look so fine crawling across the ground, licking at his own sweat.

As his pinched eyes looked up they saw the reiver band; bundles of gore and rag across the Kingdom's floor. They saw a sullen breeze pluck at their tattered clothes, and idly tug their hair.

He saw fat flies swirling amongst the dead horses, none of which had been spared in the ferocious assault. He could hear no heartbeat but his own, and that felt frail and weak in his contracted chest.

After a time he found some water and raised it to his lips, letting hot drops leak out from a small leather flask. He rubbed them on his face while he grimaced at the pain of breaths forced through his throat.

He heard a voice speaking somewhere inside his brain, and thought that it must be the voice of Kalidor. But it was the demon under ground, reaching to clutch his brain, saying, *"Unbind me. . . ."*

He was delirious and struggled to make out the words the Warrior said. The only thing Robart could understand was that if he obeyed he would be rewarded. He would have riches beyond his wildest dreams, and would slay Kalidor to become the new Dark Lord. The demon worked on him in his pyretic state, and gradually took control of him.

While Robart listened, the ships of Kalidor battled the witches' storm. The power of the magic seemed to be endless, and every ear became deafened by the roaring fury of the raging tempest and the crashing of the waves.

Black water boiled up from the churning depths below, rains fell from above, wind lashed from every point. As shafts of lightning cracked in the roiling sky they turned jet-black night into explosive day. On the Despotic Sea ruin stamped out its name for all eternity.

Waves high as mountains poured onto the plunging decks, ripping men and machines from their billets and chains. Great battlecarts went down, taking their human slaves into oblivion. Horses were swimming, men clung to clumsy rafts; masts snapped like paper twigs, sails dropped like cotton rags; and the forces of the Lord, well-drilled and dressed for war, went screaming into death.

But the fleet was a large one and its ships were well spread out, and for all its wrath and fume the storm could not survive as frenetic sorcerers on the Dark Lord's ships began flinging counterspells. There was a conflagration as powers collided, and evil went to war with spells to save the world. Across a foaming sea the dark and secret arts fought for supremacy. Kalidor himself strode on his flagship's deck, while men drowned all around and ships broke in the dark. As thunder filled the air he forced the witches' storm onto a northern path. Dripping with evil fire, blood-sweat leaking from his pores, he caught the tempest's tail and ground it in his jaws. He made the storm a rod to break across his knee, and flung it in the sea.

His men were awestruck as they gazed on his command, and saw the fire within which could control a storm. As the winds headed north they chanted out his name, and the Kingdom rang with it. This chant was *Kalidor, Defeater of the Storm!* – and men in distant lands reeled at the Dark Lord's name. He seemed invincible as he regrouped his ships, and sailed towards the east.

But the storm had blown his fleet from its intended course, and Kalidor was now far away from his old Carpathian haunts. Instead of level beach, the fleet closed on a shore of rocky points and bays. The Kingdom's armies were gathered on the cliffs, their weapons pointing down from every ridge and spur. As the look-outs sighted land it was clear that the Dark Lord's ships had found their promised war.

CHAPTER 21

Beneath a hail of stones and arrows tipped with fire, the black ships tried to land. The coastline dared them, snapping with foam-flecked jaws; great plumes of spume and spray arched up into the air. The thunder of the waves was like the battle-cry of gods beneath the sea.

The Kingdom's archers fired like possessed machines; ballistas and arbalests aimed darts hewn out of beams. Great vats of burning oil were emptied down the cliffs in sheets of flame. The black ships landed and were crushed into pulp as rocks hurled from above caused fractured cliffs to fall. Black horses strove to climb up slopes turned slick with mud, whipped on by black riders.

In those first moments ten thousand soldiers died, four hundred ships were burned and a basilisk was drowned. The sea turned red with flame, and screaming from the men formed one long endless howl. The black sky lightened as the fires created dawn, and roaring, angry waves tossed flames into the air. The grey cliffs creaked and groaned beneath the weight of men, and plunged into the sea.

Two thousand archers stood upon a storm-tossed rock, firing the poisoned darts fashioned by Kalidor. They braved a hail of fire to pick out the kings' warlords, and pierce the Kingdom's heart. As great men crashed down, clutching their wounded chests, they were bundled aside and new men took their place. The line of warriors seemed to be without end, and yet it was cut down.

Ecstatic eagles swooped down to seize their prey, ripping tongues and eyes from weary, injured men. They fought off hordes of bats which rose up from the cliffs, drawn by the Kingdom's blood. And still the ships came, pouring onto the shores, grounding on rocks and bars, gliding on beast and corpse. Black horses splashed ashore; dark swordsmen clashed their shields; drum-marshals beat tabors.

Long lines of black rats streamed from the holds of ships, spilling across the strands in an unending tide to fasten on the necks of startled warriors and tear the throats from them. Behind the black rats the flames of firedrakes could be seen blazing out across the inky tide. The pounding of their wings invoked a second storm as they lurched into the air.

The female archers of the fifth battalion found themselves set upon by wyverns from the rear. They fought heroically, using only their hands, but every one was killed.

And upon the White Rocks, where waves exploded like bombs, the retainers of the kings found that they were betrayed as their own countrymen turned round to slit their throats and toss them to the tide.

This was the way of it through the long hours of the night, as heroism fought deceit and dark despair. But by the time the dawn arrived the hordes of Kalidor had secured a beachhead.

CHAPTER 22

Far away from the smoke of war a village sorcerer worked in his humble hut. He had a black cat and a parrot, a flock of white geese and a stunted cow or two, but he was not a rich man or a great man, just an old man. He had thick white hair and a long grey beard, a sad slant to his shoulders, a jagged scar on his top lip, and dark skin weathered and pockmarked. He worked in the open air a lot, making spells for the villagers: making beans grow, making peas fat, making dogs run like wildfire, making dull, ugly girls look attractive. He was fairly content, with a few dreams remaining, though the ambitions that he had once known had faded with the years. It must have seemed from the outside that Asgarok's life was quite settled, until one evening the reiver, Robart, made a late call on him. . . .

Asgarok glanced up from his cold supper as the knock came at his door. "Who is it?" he mumbled.

"A weary traveller seeking a remedy."

"My shop is closed tonight. Can you not pick an hour somewhat more reasonable?"

"I have a long road waiting ahead of me." The tapping on the door persisted and the old man gave a sigh, shoved his plate aside and struggled to his feet.

"I'm not a young man, I need my rest," he said, reaching for the latch and pulling open the door, and with a sudden rush Robart took hold of him and held a knife to him.

"What are you doing? I don't have anything—"

Robart kicked shut the door and dragged back the old man. "I need a spell," he said. "A very ancient spell, to free a demon."

"Unbind a demon?" the old man whispered. "Such lore has been proscribed on penalty of death!"

"The law is not around, but I can give you death if that is your desire." The blade was quivering above the old man's throat, a simple thrust away from his main artery. "I can give you such a death that you will swim in it, drowning in your own blood."

"I am an old man—"

"You'll be a dead old man." The reiver bound a rope around Asgarok's wrists. "Don't even think of it, for I will cut your throat before you weave a spell." He dragged up a chair and thrust the old man down. "Just tell me what you need to raise a demon. He has been bound in spells and lies beneath the earth, chained to Kalidor."

The sorcerer trembled, reviewing all he knew about the afterlife and the life that he had now. He thought of darkness, endless oblivion, the chance that there was not an afterlife at all. After a while he took a slow, deep breath and let it whisper out. "We need a soul," he said.

Robart grunted. "What kind of soul?" he asked.

"A soul that offers itself voluntarily."

"Where will we find that soul?"

The old man's shoulders slumped. "I leave that up to you."

The reiver entered the heaving tavern just before midnight. He wore a cloak to mask his scabrous arms, and had drawn up the hood to hide his blistered face. As he shuffled through the throng he looked a traveller, left stranded for the night. He bought a mug of ale and glanced around the place, peering through veils of smoke as thick as winter mist and trying to close his ears to the clamour all around, for it distracted him. What he was looking for was the kind of lonely man who sits on the fringe of others' merriment. The kind of man who needs someone to talk to him and offer him a drink. And he could see one sitting beside the bar, a half-jug in his hand, a forced smile on his face, waiting desperately for the comely barmaid to return his smile. He was not yet eighteen, and still wore the bloom of youth, though it was getting tired beneath the ale he supped.

"This is a fine place," Robart said genially, as he stood beside the man.

"Aye, it is that," the younger man replied. "I've been here fourteen hours and never once sat down. I finished work at eight and – what day is it now?"

"This is a Tuesday."

"Oh aye, a Tuesday. I knew," the man murmured. "It's the last day for me on Old Rabunta's farm. The old man's paid me off because his new neighbour made a contraption. Do you ever believe that?" He gazed in Robart's face, and Robart saw his eyes were bleary scarlet orbs. "That you could get a thing to do the work of men, running on water power?"

Robart grunted and shook his hooded head. "These men, they just don't care. We're all just chaff to them."

"You're right," the man replied. "You're right, you're very right. We're all just chaff to them."

As the man slammed down his fist Robart clapped him on the back. "Here, have another drink. Let's have a few more drinks." He caught the landlord's eye and ordered up a jug holding six quarts of ale. . . .

Two hours later, the man, Tobian, was almost fast asleep. Robart's elbow nudged him. "That girl behind the bar—"

"Who? Sarah Rosie-Lee?" the young man mumbled.

"A very fine-looking girl."

"Oh aye, fine-looking girl. A very looking girl."

"I'll bet you like her."

"Oh aye, we all like her." Tobian screwed up his eyes and peered across the room, but all he could see by then was swirling smoke and space, as if he was lost inside a cloud. "She's a right fine-looking girl. In fact, to tell the truth, I'm half in love with her."

"And I can understand that. She seems the kind of girl a man would die for."

"Oh aye, I'd die for her," Tobian said gravely.

"You'd give your soul for her."

"I'd give my soul for her."

Robart's eyes held a gleam. "That's all I wanted to hear . . ." he muttered softly.

Upon the empty plain, beneath a blazing sun, Tobian's throat was cut. As the blood gushed onto the dusty earth, the mage called Asgarok entrapped the fleeing soul, and in an earthenware jar he mixed it with some herbs to make it quiescent. He trickled in oil, and offered up a prayer, then looked through all the books that he had brought with him, for the task of binding souls was not the kind of art that could be memorized.

"It could take years," he said.

"I'll give you two more hours." Robart cleaned off his blade, wiping away the blood, then sat down in the shade of the sorcerer's humid tent. He used a switch of grass to keep away the flies while he fiddled with his boots. He had a stone in one, and was considering that when he was king and knee-deep in his wealth, he could hire someone just to take out the pebbles.

"I'll have a boot-puller," he said to Asgarok's back, and the old man turned around and frowned in puzzlement. "To take off my new boots, because I'll have new boots on most every single day."

Asgarok nodded vaguely as he went back to his work, casting the early spells that would protect the soul; for the Dark Lord's binding chains would have defensive spells that the soul must rip apart.

"Is this a good soul?" Robart asked curiously.

"A soul is much a soul," Asgarok muttered back. "Some souls are deep and black, and this is soft and warm. That's all I can say of it."

Robart let out a long groan as he lay back in the shade, and cupped his blistered hands beneath his blistered head. "When I become king," he breathed, "I'm going to find someone to suck the blisters off."

The reiver began to drift off into a hazy sleep, where dreams of gold and power were cursed by demon fire; for what if his new lord lied and went back on his word? Where would Robart stand, then?

But the reiver trusted him, believing every word, for the Warrior controlled his thoughts, blocking out all his fears and doubts. And in a way this total lack of a mind of his own was a relief to him.

CHAPTER 23

"We must ride quickly to get to Drabnaroth," Helena murmured. She was looking anxiously towards the western sky, where the brooding smoke of war was spreading over the land. "The Dark Lord has arrived and our fate is in the hands of mortal warriors."

Helena whipped on her donkey, urging him into a trot, though it seemed a vain attempt to try to beat the pace of the oncoming war. But there was no alternative – they had to win the race to cross the Gorge. With Adam at her side she rode across the plain, cradling Raina's flame.

*   *   *

The sorcerer Asgarok looked around and wiped his hands. "The soul is primed," he said.

"Yes?" Robart sat up and dusted off his clothes. He glanced towards the west, where he could hear the drums of war. But they did not scare him now for he had found a lord who was invincible. "Is it going to work, then?"

"It says so in the book, though frankly I have doubts that this is truly wise. The demons of the earth fought for two thousand years to hold the world from men, and near succeeded. It was only the Doom Sword which claimed it back again, and only its black arts can master such dark fiends. The demon lords were born with lies upon their tongues and malice in their hearts."

"But that's my problem," said Robart casually. "Your job is just to bring this demon back again."

"He will destroy your soul."

"I will destroy your heart if you don't get on with it."

Asgarok grunted and tossed his head bravely, and Robart reached for his knife in case the mage rebelled. But deep inside his heart a curiosity was touching Asgarok. He had never done this, never performed such potent spells. He had an urge to know if it was in his power to raise up a demon, and break the ancient laws . . . he had to try this thing.

"It may not work," he said.

"It had better damn well work." Robart strode to his side and poked him in the chest. "This demon lord I serve rewards his servants well but breaks his enemies."

"I'm not his enemy," the aged mage replied. "I merely serve a force which runs through all of time."

"Quit all this mumbo stuff and set the soul to work."

"Just as you wish, Robart."

The old mage bent down and grasped the earthen jar. He tipped it on its side and wrestled out its cork. A long, unholy sigh issued from its dark heart as something grey appeared. It was like a long snake hissing and breathing fire; it coiled about the jar and crushed it into dust. Robart sprang back a pace and lifted up his sword.

"It will not harm us now." Asgarok bent down and picked up the serpent, clutching it behind its jaws, breathing into its face. He touched its yellow eyes and licked its gleaming tongue. "Now, go to work," he said. The soul arched backwards as if about to strike, and Asgarok flung it down and heeled it into the ground. It lashed about his feet, turning the soil to ash, then hurtled through the earth.

It went like lightning, carving through shale

and rock. It burst through secret caves and rivers cold and black. It ground the earth to dust and spat it out again as rivulets of flame. Down through the oceans of rock beneath the world the serpent-soul advanced upon the Dark Lord's chains. And when it ripped the bonds which bound the links in place, an earthquake hit the land. The Ancient Warrior gave a triumphant jerk, but found himself still trapped by steel bars in the earth. Watching from above, the old mage gnawed his hands.

"We need more souls . . ." he sighed.

CHAPTER 24

Lina sat waiting on a limestone bank south of Drabnaroth. She watched the dry road which wound up from the plains, at the point where it began to weave through the peaceful farms and fields. The chalk from which it was formed was dazzlingly white against the green.

A lazy river shone in the fields to the west: the sluggish Guppterol, which flowed through a small swamp before emerging again in shallow rivulets to feed Lake Malibon. The river supported great flocks of white egrets, which roosted in the fields like a blizzard on the grass. They strode amongst the herds of ox and water-deer like pale aristocrats.

Families of hop-pickers toiled in the eastern fields, stretching up to the boughs which had been crucified on stakes of twisted wood. They wore bright headscarves and leather harnesses, from which long baskets hung like babies on their backs. Children and hordes of dogs ran in and out of the stakes, shrieking excitedly.

On the north side of the hamlet the hills of Grey Devais rose up in easy waves, supporting on their backs long ranks of conifers which had been planted there. In the springtime, before the boughs thickened, the trees would be lopped down and floated through the swamp. They would form massive rafts on Lake Malibon, destined for the cities to the west.

Beyond the Grey Devais and the great Lake Malibon, the mighty Tundra Range thrust up its rugged peaks through veils of snow and mist. It was on paths through here that Lina and her group would head eventually. They would sail the Guppterol, then cross Lake Malibon, and beach at Treffick's Wharf, a loggers' camp to the north. From there, if they found a guide prepared to take them on, they would press on through the range. They would face the snowstorms and eagles of the peaks and traverse The Devil's Slide, a ridge of solid ice. They would tread narrow paths that even mountain goats would steer away from.

All this for the Doom Sword and its journey to the Fire, and their last brave attempt to thwart dark Kalidor. For the time for spells had passed, and it was time to give the world into the hands of the people.

Lina's gaze steadied as she focused on the two shapes in the distance. They were moving slowly for the donkey had gone lame, and Adam and Helena both rode on the tired Alon. The weary donkey trudged along in Alon's wake, hobbling pitifully.

They had been exhausted by the strength-devouring sun, and had bound cloths around their heads to protect their squinting eyes. They looked like desert rogues as they followed the road leading to Drabnaroth.

Lina rode to meet them, cantering on Ramadeen who kicked up trails of dust as he stretched out his legs. He snorted to a halt and a swirling cloud of chalk billowed around him. As Adam reined in the weary grey, Alon, a bright and happy smile broke over Lina's face. She felt a great relief that he'd come to no harm, other than some cuts and bumps.

"You look abysmal," she said.

Adam grinned back at her. "It was quite a trek," he said. "We battled sandstorms, and got stung by hordes of wasps."

"I've had a lazy time."

"Yes, I can tell," he said. "But mine's the better tan."

"Your tan is lobster-red."

"Never mind this clap-trap." Helena struggled to climb from Alon's back, kicking at her flapping skirt which had wrapped itself around her pack. "Did you find that Pignikker?"

"Yes."

"Was he sober?"

"Almost," said Lina.

"Pah!" Helena snorted as she dusted down her clothes, slapping her long brown skirt as if she hated it. "Has he acquired a boat?"

"He said he'll look for one."

"Looking is not good enough." Helena straightened, and squinted down the lane. "Where is the drunken fool?"

"Sleeping inside a barn."

"*Sleeping inside a barn?*" The witch's eyes narrowed. "I'll soon sort him out." She strode off muttering an assortment of threats and curses while Adam slowly eased himself out of Alon's hot saddle, the sword still on his back.

"It's good to see you again."

"It's good to see you, too," Lina said happily.

CHAPTER 25

After a night spent in the hay-loft of a barn on the edge of Drabnaroth they gathered up their things early the next morning, and headed through the town. The day was balmy, with a roseate hue and cotton-candy clouds drifting across the sky. A breeze out of the east spoke of the wild lemon groves it had wandered through.

They left the horses to graze Pignikker's field and passed through a flock of swallows which scooped flies from the grass. They heard a cuckoo sing from a cracked hawthorn stump beside a woodcock's nest.

Beyond a small burn they stopped to check their packs when the ruddy Pignikker complained that he'd lost his hat. He kicked up quite a fuss until the hat appeared inside his back pocket. He was a small middle-aged man, stocky and hairy-armed, as if to compensate for a fast-balding scalp, and he had a gravel voice which complained constantly at Helena's treatment of him. The pair went "way back", he boasted frequently, although he never said what linked them. Lina said he must have been Helena's beau, but when the witch overheard her look was withering.

All four were in good heart, and the thing which most cheered them was that Helena had at last found time to create a shielding cloak. With the cloak wrapped around the Doom Sword, the chances of somebody following them had been greatly reduced, and a crushing weight seemed to have been lifted from their tired shoulders.

They headed westwards to the banks of the Guppterol, where a flat-bottomed rowing boat had been drawn up amongst a thick stand of swaying willowherb, and Pignikker looked on proudly.

"I had a lot of trouble getting hold of this boat, you know."

"Shut up," said Helena, who was unable to talk to Pignikker without giving the impression that she was utterly and almost insanely bored by him. But she helped him load up the small craft, and they shoved it clear of the mud which hugged the crowded bank, scattering the heaving shoals of tiny brown minnows which thronged the shallow water.

When they had all climbed aboard they used long punting poles to push away the boat into the sluggish stream, and then the current took over, easing them downriver. It was still very early; the only sign of life was a farmer in his fields. As the river's speed increased they used the punting poles to hold the boat on its course.

By the middle of the afternoon they had left the fields behind, and were heading through flat country. The hills of the Grey Devais were moving closer, but so was the acrid smell of the swamp which lay ahead. To either side of the river there were long tracts of mud, which grumbled quietly. The day grew humid, and clouds of insects swarmed as the pleasant breeze of dawn turned into sluggish air. They were now constantly brushing sweat from their brows.

The river had begun to break up into a web of streams which wandered through tall banks of reeds and bulrushes. Long, muddy islands loomed, crowned by thick mangrove plants which trailed their roots like stilts. Fish eagles watched them from perches in the trees. Caymans slipped from the banks to submerge in rippling pools. Dragonflies prowled the reeds like angry prison guards, checking no bugs emerged. There was a smell of swamp gas so pure and dense that to ignite a flame would have been foolhardy.

"This smell disgusts me," muttered Helena.

Pignikker liked it.

They raised a canopy to divert the gnats, and Helena smouldered herbs which would have destroyed an ox. But the buzzing insect hordes seemed to be oblivious and devoured the herbs.

As the streams grew broader and flatter in the swamp they had to use the poles to guide them through the reeds. By the time evening came they were almost entrapped in stinking, fuming ooze.

"This is the swampland," Pignikker remarked dismally.

"Get out and pull," the witch said callously.

With some reluctance their guide jumped over the side, where he sank up to his waist in the fetid, clinging mud. With a rope wrapped round his chest he pulled on the small boat, groaning pathetically. He had to suffer snake bites as well as admonishments from the witch, who seemed convinced that he was feigning injury. After a time she lit a brand to make things easier, and Pignikker forged ahead.

The swampland petered out through the alluvial shores surrounding Malibon. This was a vast lake stretching from west to east, with a thousand islands scattered down its length. In parts it was so deep that neither mage nor man could estimate its floor. It had once held huge shoals of fish and silver-squid, but they had been so pillaged that most clung to the deeps, and each year more fishermen from the huts along the shore packed up their nets and left.

Most of the islands were uninhabited, though strange rumours were attached to some of them. It was said that in the night one could hear voices or see dim, shifting lights. But they were mostly sanctuaries or exploration sites, where miners dug for gold and hollowed out the rock. There were large settlements on the two main isles, to the west of Treffick's Wharf.

By the time Adam's group reached the shoreline, having dragged their boat for the last half league, darkness had filled the sky, and they set up their camp in a beached, rusting hulk.

At night great hunting owls with a taste for human flesh patrolled the dark currents a stone's throw from the shore, and they built a roaring fire to keep the birds at bay and shred the hovering gloom. They listened to the water owls and otters in the reeds, and the whispers of low waves as they splashed against the shore. They heard a distant bell, and saw the far-off lights of a ship heading for port.

But over all of this hung a dark, unbroken sky, as black as any tomb which might be found in Hell. The night seemed oddly tense, as if the lake could sense that the Doom Sword was abroad.

CHAPTER 26

At dawn the next morning they pushed off from shore with their long, unwieldy poles. They had a day's sailing before they reached Treffick's Wharf, and the breeze which filled their cloth seemed in a fretful mood. There was no time to waste, and they ate as they travelled.

The course they were taking would pass between two isles, both unusually large and covered with dense plant growth. Though both teemed with wildlife and had sheltered bays, nobody lived on them. It was said that the larger one held the tombs of long-dead kings, and the smaller had been cursed by a pestilential plague. Small towns which once had thrived had become overgrown by choking weeds and vines.

But the party had no intention of setting foot on either isle, for their course lay straight ahead, between the main currents. If they wandered from their path they would stand a reasonable chance of encountering vortices. So Helena held a lodestone to give a compass guide, and Pignikker lashed an oar to the stern to act as a rudder. In this way they proceeded without incident until the afternoon. And then a mist appeared, drifting across the lake and shrouding the two large isles which were now flanking them. They seemed to sail within a narrow, white ravine, over which towered sheer slate cliffs which gabled both the isles, and as the mist rolled in, banking and thickening, their route became impenetrable. Iron ore within the cliffs affected the black lodestone, so that they lost their course and had to drop the sail. As the boat cruised slowly on, they heard the splash of waves slapping against the rocks.

They glided slowly into the small sheltered bay which scarred the smaller isle. They could not continue without a clearer route, for whirl-pools lay ahead, where the lake's main currents met. And the mist was now so dense that the sun itself was hidden from their gaze. They could only wait gloomily, sitting on the chunks of slate which had crashed from the slopes which reared above their heads. The beach was lined with stones, and the lake was still and black. The dank air chilled their bones.

On the island, the goddess Barognigod, who made the swirling mists, had long been restless. She was not a true goddess, except to those who served, who thought Barognigod had made the sky and earth; but she could seem a goddess when she drew on her veils and stretched her sundry limbs. She could strike terror into a mortal eye, and paralyse her foes with one slash of her fangs. For several thousand years she had sat on the isle, patiently waiting.

The Feylan who attended her, little more advanced than apes, had toiled for centuries to cater to her whims. They had offered dogs and goats, horses and squealing men to please her appetite. But there was one thing which Barognigod desired, and which they had never found through all their servitude. The goddess Barognigod wanted to suck the flame out of a human soul.

Now at last she sensed one, through its rare, elusive light: a trembling patch of blue glowing inside the fog. Her flexing limbs quivered as they sensed Raina's warmth, and her long fangs dripped with gore.

From her mist-draped fortress she issued her command: *"Bring back this flame or you will surely die. And slaughter every man who would stand in your way, and bring their flesh to me."*

She gave the Feylan sleep-dust to sprinkle in the travellers' eyes, and long, exquisite blades with which to slit their throats. She gave them silver bowls in which to place the hearts they would cut from the chests.

She offered promises of freedom and reward when this last task was done. She said they would sail away across the open lake.

Their dark goddess lied to them.

As evening settled the mist still showed no sign of lifting. The party had begun to explore the isle, seeking a place to camp, resigned to having lost half a day's travelling. Their hope was that the night would clear away the mist, so that they could leave at dawn.

They found a clearing a short way from the bay, where several ancient trees had been felled by a storm. There they spread out their packs, but it was a gloomy gathering. Even the camp fire burned with a subdued glow, as if it too was numbed by the moisture in the air. The sounds of the night seemed weirdly dull and vague, blanketed by the fog.

Pignikker strode off to gather extra wood.

Helena tried a lifting spell, but rather mutedly. Lina lay by her pack, staring into the fire, a blanket wrapped round her.

As it neared midnight Adam walked to the bay, unable to sleep or settle on the ground. He stood and tossed stones into the water, hearing each one go down, but seeing none of them. His mood was cheerless and a million miles removed from the passion of the dawn, where all had seemed possible. Now the members of his group, the Doom Sword, Kalidor – all seemed but fleeting dreams. He felt mortality as he gazed out on the lake: the thought that all things die, and all things disappear. He was in a very gloomy state when he turned from the shore and wandered back again.

When he got back to the camp, the beasts of night were already crouching atop his friends. The Feylan were dark and stunted, and their fangs dripped with green saliva. Their blazing yellow eyes flickered with poisoned fire. Their powerful, hirsute hands clutched his friends around their throats, squeezing the life from them. But no one fought back, for sleep-dust was in their eyes, bringing troubled dreams through which dark monsters loomed. His friends knew that they were dying, but could not drag themselves out of their nightmares.

Adam gave a startled cry as he ran into the

glade, picking a flaming brand from the half-sleeping fire. Swinging it round his head he drove away the beasts, but their laughter mocked at him. It was as if a phantasm still lingered in the glade long after the Feylan left, bearing Raina's soul. It was like the sounds of bats clattering amongst the trees which fringed the flickering grove. There was something evil about the twittering notes, and they cut through Adam's nerves, making his body shake. He grabbed the sleeping witch, but she would not waken, no matter how he cried.

He ran to Pignikker, who was blue in the face, and screamed in Lina's ear, straining to pick her up. Then he saw the witch's open pack, and a dark yawning void where Raina's lamp should be.

He heard the black beasts escaping through the trees, heard their grunts and snorts as they discussed their raid. They were fading into the night as he reached for his shielding cloak and pulled out the Doom Sword.

CHAPTER 27

The Dark Lord Kalidor stood on the bloody cliffs as the last of his foes died. They died in torment, their hearts ripped from their breasts. They died with purple tongues as their breath was denied. They died in shame and rage, knowing that they had failed to hold back the grim hordes.

Already the armies of night were pouring over the bloodstained cliffs, dragging away their battlecarts and weapons, their mighty steam machines, their storming sledgehammers, the contrivances of war. Black hounds in cages were hauled up from the deep; the horses of the lance re-formed as cavalry. Fell beasts which had no name were unleashed from their chains to scout across the land. Dragons and manticores, harpies and witheralls – all creatures of the dark were called to lend support. In long, unbroken lines which tore down all before them, they streamed over the plains.

Adam sprinted through the obstructing trees, hacking to right and left to clear himself a path, clutching the cold Doom Sword in a two-handed grip, stark terror in his chest. His face was frozen in a tense grimace, and he prayed desperately for the sword to come alive. But it stayed silent within his shaking hands; it did not flash or pulse, but was only a blade; and Adam needed it to give him strength and hope, to feel its awesome power.

He crossed a wide river, splashing through its chilling flow, slipping across flat stones which looked like grey tombstones. He scrambled up a bank where long thorns slashed his hands and branches whipped his face. But his prey stayed up ahead of him, moving away from him, their voices fading out into the dense jungle. As fast as Adam ran he could not gain a stride upon the fleet creatures.

He reached a defile, and a slick precipitous path which plunged down through the rock into a wide basin where little vegetation grew.

It was mere empty space, filled with the trunks of trees and dry, dead branches. The mist had lifted and the moon came shining through, lighting up grey rocks which had been polished smooth and long strands of thick white filaments which hung between the trees. It was as if cotton wool had been spread over the boughs, drooping in silvered sheets like breath hung out to dry. It stuck like candy floss as Adam cleared the threads, following Raina's flame.

The air turned chilly and the moment dream-like as Adam walked through gloom, picking up clinging threads. He was surrounded by stark trees and smooth, grey, brooding rocks. Darkness lay up ahead. It was as if he was in a cavern dragged to the open air, and the silence filling it was bristling and intense. He found himself slowing down to a more wary pace. Something was living here, he felt quite sure, as sure as he had ever been of anything. He did not know it yet, but he had entered the lair of the grim Barognigod.

The goddess trembled as her faithful slaves brought her the lantern. They advanced on all fours, in jerkins of black hide, their faces turned to the earth to avoid her blazing eyes. They made the sign of a cross upon their barrel chests, and muttered fervent prayers. Two of them chanted canticles and fingered rosaries, and every several steps stooped down to kiss the ground that their all-powerful goddess might deign to walk upon.

One killed a chicken and spread about its blood, splashing the thick white strands which dogged their every step, for the threads were everywhere, and had resolved themselves into a sprawling web. Its span covered ten hectares, and at the heart of it lurked the great Feylan queen, the multi-legged beast, the witch with poisoned fangs, the spider Barognigod.

The high priest set down the glowing lantern on a rock altar. He wore a long cassock fashioned from gore-stained cloth, and a stole of thick white fur filched from an arctic fox. A band about his head was formed of oryx hoof, ground down and mixed with blood. He held a crucible in which he offered the blood, drawn from the youngest child in the Feylans' treetop camp. He poured it on the rock and spread it with his hands, like a sticky, crimson tar.

When the blood had dried he stepped away again, murmuring the sacred words of a long-forgotten tongue. He knew them by heart, but had no idea what he was talking about. They were the words that Selibu, their ancient king, had heard when he once led the Feylan tribe towards its promised land – a journey which fell foul of plunderers from the north, who forced them to the isle.

As his words went whispering through the darkness of the grove, the high priest felt a tremor run throughout the strands. The queen Barognigod was stirring in her cave, testing her hunger. She had already brushed aside her thoughts of warming flesh, for there was greater fare to please her appetite. She savoured with delight the thought of her black fangs devouring Raina's soul. It was the taboo, the Act Which Bore No Name – the taking of a soul bought by another's death; to have their thoughts and dreams, their very spark of life, for all eternity. It was said that only Rugzudik, the demon of the south, had dared to break the vows protecting human souls, but as the massive spider-beast stirred on her bed of skulls, she planned to be the next.

Adam halted at the edge of the sacred grove where the Feylan slaves fed their obscene goddess. The air was foul-smelling, for the trees were draped with skin and tatters of dried flesh hung down, half-putrefied. The smell crept down his throat as if it planned to stay. It made his skin prickle, and the hairs on his neck stiffened uncomfortably.

He searched for the Feylan, but the apes had

disappeared, for they were not allowed to watch Barognigod feed. They had vanished into the trees, picking their way between the globules of her slime. All that Adam could see now was the lantern on the rock, and the fallen crucible which the priest had overlooked. He saw no sign of life, heard no approaching threat, and yet he sensed something. It was a trembling in the awesome lint-like web, a sense of something huge moving a long way off. As he jumped down to the floor of the silent stinking grove, he heard the goddess approach.

Almost immediately the Doom Sword sprang to life, and tongues of pale blue flame flickered along its length. Adam caught a fleeting glimpse of gleaming, distant plates, scraping like lizard scales.

He took a quick step, but he had been caught by the threads, which fastened to his soles like limpets on a rock. As he swung the Doom Sword down it seemed to change to fire, burning straight through the strands. He took another step but became bogged down again, this time by stronger threads, by fiercer balls of slime. This time the Doom Sword's thrust took fractionally more time to burn away the threads.

He struggled onwards towards Raina's flame, slashing through the threads, walking, becoming trapped. Each time he took a step more threads clung to his feet and wrapped about his legs. He was becoming ever more encircled by the clutches of the web, trapped like a fly. As Adam's tension rose so the actions of the sword became more cumbersome. It was almost howling as he tried to pull it free from a thick, clinging mass of twisted threads and slime. As he glanced up in alarm, he saw the shifting bulk of the beast come through the trees.

He held the Doom Sword stiffly ahead of him as the great goddess appeared. She was enormous, and seemed to fill his sight. Her outer covering glowed with a blue-bronze light. She was covered with scales of adamant and iron. Her eyes were ruby fire. Though she moved ponderously, with well-selected steps, the goddess crossed the earth with terrifying speed. She was a tower of legs and eyes and jaws scuttling through the grove. Trees bent before her, rocks cracked beneath her feet, the grove shook like a drum beaten by mighty fists. With her came the musty, sickly stench of the cavern of death where she devoured her kills. The stink of limbs and bones garnered across the years leaked from Barognigod's pores.

As the goddess neared Adam she revealed acid fangs: long spears of skin and bone sharpened to gleaming points. Bright beads of venom glowed, then dripped to the earth, hissing like poisoned rain. As she loomed over him, her massive spinnerets threw off silver threads as thick as ships' hawsers, which she cast through the air like glistening fishing lines tossed to a distant carp.

The goddess circled, watching Adam's pulsing sword as if it posed the threat of an unfamiliar prey. She swayed to right and left, and thrust out cautious strands as if to test the blade.

While this was happening, Adam stood motionless, afraid to move his feet in case they bound him more; but he could feel the pale Doom Sword begin to thrum with power and flicker warningly. He was close by the lantern, and could hear Raina's soul urging him to beware the spider's sudden strike. As her voice filled his ears, the spider made a lunge, feinting first to the right.

Adam struck upwards, landing a ringing blow which glanced back from the plates the gleaming spider wore. A bead of poison dripped and burned through his white shirt, searing into his flesh. As Adam ripped off his shirt to toss it at the beast, he sought a softer spot beneath her carapace. But the spider kept moving, circling around again, lunging and darting back.

Adam's gaze followed her as he turned on the spot, the strands of silken rope winding around his legs until he was quite bound in a white half-cocoon which stretched up to his waist. His only hope now lay in the pulsing sword, which had aroused itself to counteract the threat. The sword and Adam moved, their tension intertwined, their anger one black rage.

The spider disgusted them and her smell offended them; her posturing displays seemed merely arrogance. Adam was on the brink of bringing down a goddess, and he could sense it now. He felt immortal, protected by the sword; nothing could bring him harm, nothing could stand in his way. Inside a blaze of light he hacked away the strands which trapped him.

He was almost snarling as he advanced towards the beast, raising aloft the sword, scattering flames and sparks. The spider backed away, confused and disarrayed, as Adam lunged at her. He swung a savage blow which whistled through the air and sliced down through the plate which shielded one long leg. The spider's body jerked as her limb was severed, and dropped down to the ground. She darted forward, flinging herself on the youth, spitting out poisoned rain to sear and blind his eyes. She flattened out her legs to crush down with her weight as he closed in to strike.

Adam stabbed her brutally, driving with all his strength, plunging his singing blade into her dark belly. He prised apart the plates and hacked into her flesh, watching her thick blood flow. As the goddess sprang back, stunned and bemused, astonished at her pain, confused by all her blood, Adam spoke. "I give you life," he said, "when I could cut you down and make a corpse of you. I could destroy you."

Adam held aloft the sword, and the goddess saw its blade shimmer and flash with bursts of blue and silver light.

"This is the Doom Sword which nothing can resist, and nothing will survive." The goddess wilted before the swaying blade, sensing the power within, and the rage which drove Adam. As he picked up the lantern she watched him out of eyes which glimmered fearfully.

While Adam backed off he watched her carefully, but she was not about to make a challenge now, for the goddess Barognigod saw that there are greater powers than even gods possess. She would have to content herself with mindless Feylan slaves, eating the blood and corpses they served up to her, knowing that she was alone in a dark, empty cave, trapped by her solitude. . . .

Adam returned to the clearing in which his friends still slept and blew the magic dust from their eyes. He built up the fire in case the Feylan came, and sat protecting them, with the sword across his knees. He waited till dawn, when his friends awoke and looked round puzzled. Helena questioned him on all that had transpired, and made him wrap the sword inside its shielding cloak. During the time it was in use it would have drawn the eye of every Kingdom beast. This meant that Kalidor would now know where they were and, even more than that, could estimate their course. He would be making plans to intercept the group before they reached the gorge.

So time was vital, and they kicked out the fire, shoved afloat the boat and threw their packs aboard; and as the sun rose above Lake Malibon they sailed off to the north. It was a clear day and the mist had disappeared, and the islands at their rear looked as serene as dreams. There was no sound at all from the goddess Barognigod or her faithful Feylan slaves.

PART 3

The Bridge of Doom

CHAPTER 28

The smoke of Treffick's Wharf circled above the town like a grey halo. It was a logging town, built round its timber mills which spewed out endless streams of staves to fence the world. Buzzing saws roared day and night like angry bluebottles. It was also a gathering place for trappers from the hills, who met in its muddy streets to discuss recent kills, and stood round blazing fires with their dogs at their feet and their mules at their sides.

A wooden jetty extended from the town, far out into the lake where low-slung barges lurked, loading up furtively as if they felt ashamed to rob the forest's heart. A seething mass of logs jostled along the shore, like beasts awaiting slaughter.

As Pignikker steered the boat between the low barges, men working on the decks waved to him. They seemed to know the man, and he was waving back in pleased acknowledgement. Only the grey witch appeared not to be pleased that they had reached the Wharf without further mishap, but her thoughts were moving on, beyond the logging town, to the white peaks behind. It would be the final stage of their journey to the gorge, with only the Bridge of Doom to cross to reach the Eternal Fire. But Kalidor would know where the group was heading now, and would be waiting.

News had spread quickly about the Dark Lord's advance from the despairing cliffs on which his troops had fought. Nothing could slow them down, nothing could turn them back, they seemed invincible. They crossed the Kingdom in an unholy tide, driving their poisoned flags into each slaughtered land. No force of man or beast could withstand their advance, and the grey witch felt afraid. If Kalidor took the Doom Sword all of the world would be his, and they were just four souls against his rampant hordes. So she stared beyond the town, into the grim dark hills where lay their destiny.

*   *   *

"Helena," Adam asked quietly, "why do you hate Pignikker?"

Helena stirred herself and stared back at Adam. "Why do you ask me that? I don't hate Pignikker."

"You're never kind to him. You never answer him. And he really worships you."

Helena snorted and looked back down the boat to where the stocky figure of Pignikker crouched, holding his rudder-oar. "He is a fool," she said, "who should love other things than futile, ageing crones."

"Do you think he loves you?"

"Oh yes," the grey witch said. "He has been in love with me for far too many years, more than we can now recall – since we were tiny babes running across the fields of our far distant home."

Adam was puzzled. "But you are older than him."

"Only on my face, for we share the same old hearts. I once gave him a gift which turned into a curse, and yet he still loves me for it." She gave a great sigh, as though inside her mind she was casting far back to those dim distant times. "We were little fools who thought the world was ours. We lived in Herringport, a village on the coast, not far from Kalidor's fort upon the Carpath hills—"

"Did you know Kalidor?"

"Oh yes, he was our lord and we his servants." Helena sat back and smoothed her tangled hair, gazing down at the lake and her reflection. "He was a carpenter, and I the village witch, and oh, the times we had—" She smiled at Adam, with eyes lost in the past, eyes which were grey and soft and on the point of tears. "Of all the men I've known I loved Pignikker best, but it could never be. All of my sisters – they used to tease," she cried. "They called him *man of stone*, and other foolish things. But he was very kind, and suffered all their jibes as if they flattered him."

She went on, "When we were seventeen we made a foolish pact – that we would never part and we would love so hard, so long, so true, so deep, that none could come between." The witch's vision clouded as she looked on a past now darkened with the fears and loss that there had been; for no one has a past complete and without doubts; no one has everything. "One dark man did come, the grim Lord Kalidor, who wanted simple spells to make his fat face fair, and as a childish prank I put a massive wart upon his crooked nose."

"He would have killed you."

"He nearly did," she said. "It was only Pignikker who got me out of town, hidden inside a cask in which they brewed up ale which I still taste sometimes. So I had to leave then, and go up into the hills, while Pignikker remained behind to cover up my trail. And we did not meet again until several years had elapsed, and the war had started."

The small boat juddered as a bow-wave picked it up and drenched it with the wash of a fast-steaming barge. Pignikker righted it and grunted out a curse which Adam strained to hear.

"The war was terrible, and all looked on death and saw no compromise and no immunity. We all prepared to die, and in our separate ways tried to make terms with it. We were in a small cave, Pignikker and myself, when the hordes of Kalidor came sweeping through the land. They were going to burn us out and, in a wild moment, I spoke a desperate prayer. Pignikker made me do so, for we thought that we would die, and I performed a spell that we might never change, but would stay as we were, so young, so full of life, blessed with our inner fire. The spell took hold of us, but before it was complete I had to flee the cave, for I sighted Kalidor. But Pignikker remained, and alone was doomed to stay at that age ever more. Young without me," she said, staring in Adam's eyes. "For I grow old and grey, and am destined to die. But when he looks on me he still sees that young woman who cast a spell on him."

"But if he still loves you—"

"He loves a dream," she said. "He loves the girl I was, and the young woman I became. He does not see the lines, the hair, the face, the looks – only my memory."

"No, he sees you," said Adam. "The one he wants to see. The woman that he loved, the one he always will. Such love is complete because it never pales."

"And you know this?" she said.

"I know he loves you," Adam said bluntly.

Helena looked away, adjusting her grey shawl, noticing that their boat had almost berthed beside the wooden wharf. "And you love Raina's soul, while there's a girl back there who is in love with you." She stood up suddenly to cast a landing rope, while Adam's eyes looked back to where the huntress sat. She was all on her own, staring across the lake, lost in a reverie.

CHAPTER 29

The hordes of Kalidor, on their unstoppable march, slaughtered the Kingdom. They cut down farmers and mighty warriors, young women in the fields, their children in their arms. They burned down homes and inns, set fire to meeting halls, ignited timber yards. They raided vineyards and warehouses of grain, stampeded herds of ox and poisoned the ground. They pulled down every tree, set fire to every flag, tore roofs from every home. A swathe of murder came walking in their wake; outriders rode ahead seeking for further prey. Nothing dulled their advance, no archers slowed them down, no ramparts broke their stride.

The Dark Lord Kalidor was thunder in their midst,

*riding a jet-black steed caparisoned with fire. He bore
a sword of fire which was so drenched with blood its
flame outshone the sun. He wore a hauberk fashioned
from human skin, a shield formed from bone,
gauntlets made of souls. His boots dripped with the
blood of those he walked upon in his untamed
advance. He had seen the Doom Sword flash upon
the distant isle as Adam pulled the blade from its
protective cloak, and knowing which way it went,
knowing its goal, he moved to head it off.*

*No force opposed him, for most men were now dead
along the western flanks of the lands through which
he rode. The only thing which moved was the flag he
left behind, tossed by a lonely wind.*

The mountain guide that Pignikker had arranged
met them on the quayside. He was a tall man
from the northern provinces, who could have
hidden hens inside his mane of hair. He had
a tangled beard as black as ravens' wings. His
eyes were dark as coal.

He met them cheerfully. "My name is Bulribar
and I am very strong – stronger than an ox."

"I can see that, Bulribar," said the grey witch
quietly, as she checked his massive arms.

"I can rip out trees!" he cried.

"Good, we'll bear that in mind if we find trees
to rip." She turned to Pignikker. "Where did
you find this man?"

"He was all I could get," he said.

"I see." Helena turned back to face the mountain man, so completely dwarfed by him that her eyes stared at his belt. "Do you know these mountains well?"

"Like the back of my hand. My name is *Bulribar!*" He rolled the syllables, as if he loved the name, and Helena was forced to ask him what his great name meant. "It means 'he who eats the bull'!"

"I see. How very quaint," responded Helena.

The travellers spent that evening inside a tavern in the centre of the town. Hoping for privacy, they were a little disconcerted when the mighty mountain man called over all his friends, and in a drunken haze introduced each one of them, with all their virtues.

"This one is Prapplegraff, who can spit up a tree and knock down a pigeon!"

"How very quaint that is," the witch said patiently. "How very quaint indeed."

"And this is Brobag, who ate a snake so long its head popped out of him before its tail was gone! It took him several days."

"And I am not surprised," the witch said quietly.

"This one is Grubatol—"

"Who once married a bear?"

"How did you know that?" Bulribar stared dumbfounded. "Have you two met before?"

"It was a lucky guess," the grey witch mumbled.

"I see. Well, never mind," the mountain man went on. "This one is Pusbucket—"

And so it went on, right through his twenty friends, but in the middle of it all Adam and Lina slipped away down to the dock, and sat on the stones, staring across the lake.

It was a still night and the moonlight was intense, turning Lake Malibon into a silver shield. They could see the distant lights of trawlers heading back to port, with mostly empty nets. They could smell thick wood-smoke from bonfires in the streets, and hear long lines of dogs fighting for scraps of meat. They caught the dismal sound of a bell announcing that a prayer service would start immediately.

Someone was fishing from the lipped end of the dock with a long, curving rod. He had a friend with him who had long since given up and curled into a heap. They heard faint honking from geese coming home to roost and the sound of scrappy fights as drunken trappers met. And over all of this was the sound of the great sawmills, buzzing into the night.

It all seemed a long way from the war with Kalidor, and the thought that one day soon this town might be destroyed. The trappers would disappear, slaughtered or fled to the hills, and the loggers would be gone.

"What do you think will happen when this is over?" Adam asked quietly.

"I don't know." Lina sighed, then pulled a chunk of wood out of a rotting pile and tossed it into the lake. She watched the ripples spread until they disappeared, then tossed another. "We'll defeat Kalidor, for with the Doom Sword gone he will lose his desire and much of his black power. He will be sent to his isle, and the towers will be rebuilt to watch over him. And the darkness will go back to the place from which it came, and harmony will rule until another sword – or something just as bad – comes out of someone's heart and threatens us again."

"Will it be like that for ever?"

"Maybe. I cannot know, I'm not a soothsayer."

Adam shifted on the greasy dock, staring down at the stones which lay beneath his feet. "And what of you?" he asked. "What are you going to do when this is over?"

"I'll go back home," she said. "Go back to hunt the deer and dream of Kalidor." She gave a long sigh. "And what will you do then? Will you stay in the north or travel to the south?"

"To the place where we met?"

"That's where I'm going to be," Lina said softly. She took a deep breath. "If you ever needed me – if you were all alone and looking for a friend—" She looked away from him, and glanced up at the stars. "You could come home with me."

"I have my own home," Adam said quietly, though he had no idea how to get back to it. Perhaps the Doom Sword knew, perhaps Helena knew. "If I can get back to it."

"And do you have friends there? A friend as good as me?"

"I have no friends like you. No one as good as you."

Adam took Lina's hand as they stared at the lake, watching the ships sail home.

CHAPTER 30

Che Ancient Warrior burst from his rocky grave and roared across the world. He had shed his bindings, and battled through the earth, clawing towards the sky like a creature possessed. He had been helped in this by all the slaughtered souls Asgarok had sacrificed. Now, naked and wounded, he stood upon the earth, burned by the wizards' chains, scarred by the savage rock. Noticing Asgarok, and fearing sorcerers, he promptly slew him.

"Where is this dark place?"

"The Plain of Albadroth." The reiver Robart knelt to greet his risen lord.

"And where is my black horse?"

"The horse has disappeared into oblivion. I have another horse—"

The Warrior glanced at it, curling his blackened lips in a display of scorn. "I do not want that horse. Bring me a silver beast from the herd of Dornok."

"The herd of Dornok?"

"It is several days away."

"I know where it is, my lord," Robart said gloomily. "Do you want me to ride there now?"

"What are you waiting for? We have no time to waste."

The reiver stood up and climbed on his horse, a little aggrieved that he had not been better praised. He had toiled long and hard . . . But maybe demon lords reward in other ways. "I'll fetch a horse, then."

Robart rode off through the night, leaving the Warrior to slump in waves of weariness, for it was exhausting work defeating wizards' spells, and he was not recovered yet. It could take him several days, and it is never fit to let a slave observe his master's weaknesses. The first law of a lord is *Keep your slaves occupied*. When he had recovered he would resume the search, knowing that the Doom Sword's trail would have turned cold by now. But a weapon like the sword, which pulsed with power, could not stay cold for long.

Using the slaughtered mage as a pillow for his head, he settled in the dirt to let his strength return. He would rest a little while, recover from his wounds, then let his rage commence. He would take the reiver Robart as a slave to serve his whims, and when he had tired of him he would eat his still-warm heart. Servants had other ways of pleasing their grim lords than merely fetching steeds.

CHAPTER 31

Early next morning the band departed Treffick's Wharf, leading a line of mules. They had provisions to last them for three weeks, although the journey itself should take only six days, but it would be foolhardy to under-estimate the threat from the Tundra Range. Many climbers and hunters had been lost on the exposed slopes, destroyed by avalanche or killed by frost and wolves. Many had lost their way, and some had disappeared into the jaws of the Logra – a creature born of myth, a rolling ball of fire which swept down from the peaks. But the Logra's existence was not the travellers' main concern, for their thoughts were moving on to the task which lay ahead. If they survived this trek they would reach the Bridge of Doom and confront Kalidor.

He was the final obstacle between them and their goal, the force they must defeat to reach the Eternal Fire. Against a man like that the Logra's rolling fire seemed quite a small affair.

The day dawned peacefully, with a warm breeze on the air and a sky untouched by cloud. The rolling foothills of the brooding Tundra Range took them above the town at a fairly rapid pace, so that by late morning it was no more than a blur on the shores of Lake Malibon. They could still see the smoke rise, but the sound of the sawmills had gone, as had the shouts and barks from the small town's bustling streets. Beyond, Lake Malibon was a long, bright mirror, facing the glaring sun.

When they cleared the next ridge the town and lake were gone, and they were in empty, silent hills where once great forests bloomed before the loggers came to rip them from the earth. The loggers were now looking eastwards for new supplies of trees, leaving nothing but scars upon the gentle slopes. Buzzards patrolled the air, as if still searching for the perches they'd once known.

Some leagues ahead of the band the slopes began to rise into the sheer rock walls of the

Tundra Range proper, where ibexes and goats clung to precarious nooks above the discomfiting drops. If the group got that far, they would then enter the mists which circled the Tundra Range in a cold, grey girdle. Then thick frosts would begin, spreading up to the peaks with their mantles of snow. After another two days they would reach the Devil's Slide, a straight expanse of ice which had claimed many lives. After that they would have to cross the racing Zinniga Ford, and they would be safely home – assuming that the Zinniga race was in a friendly mood, and that its zander-shark were in a peaceful state. And that the Barberi tribe were engaged in things other than guarding their domain. . . .

The air turned progressively colder as the party followed the winding trails through the silent grey hills, with only patrolling hawks and the odd distant wolf to keep them company. The empty sky had a metallic hue, and the yellow sun looked thin and anaemic. The air felt rarefied, though they had barely started their climb to the peaks. The massive Slyne Bank still lay ahead of them, a relic of the war when demons had gained control, and in a desperate bid to outmanoeuvre them men had raised up earthworks. They were a diversion to lure in the demons, and brave men sacrificed themselves to make the decoy work. Some twenty thousand souls were lost while even braver souls fought to reach the demon king. Such exploits ripple through the land's chronology: tales of the heroes gone and those who went before. The Kingdom's past is proud, and it still honours its dead with proper privilege.

The mood of the travellers became more sombre as they settled into the dull routine of goading stubborn mules. There was little talking, and even Raina's soul seemed to burn with less heat and not so bright a flame. She had been quiet and pale since leaving Treffick's Wharf, for Raina sensed a change. Adam and Lina shared close affection now, and the driving warmth of it was outshining Raina's lamp. She could sense Adam drifting from her towards Lina's mortal arms, leaving her flame behind.

Maybe Raina's sadness was an infectious thing, for by early afternoon their line was well strung out, and each was lost in thoughts that no one else could share, or even realize.

"We are a sad lot," said Bulribar gravely, to the grey witch Helena.

Helena looked up from Raina's glowing lamp, and wrapped it in a fold of cloth across her lap. "It is the time of year. It is the time of life. The time for many things."

Bulribar grunted. His mule was so weighed

down it was almost staggering as he shifted on its back. "I know that some things are still eternal. The Tundra never change."

Helena glanced up to the white mountains overhead, so pure against the sky they looked beyond all harm. "Even the peaks will fall if Kalidor succeeds and gains the Doom Sword."

"Oh, ha! The Doom Sword!" Bulribar gave a snort. "A thing of childish dreams – there never was a sword. And as for Kalidor, who is this upstart lord? He'll never get this far. War will not come up here. We are just simple men hunting the deer and lynx." Bulribar look around, surveying his domain, and for a moment his rugged face looked as though it could stop war. But even he could sense that in these changing times nothing was sacrosanct. "War will not come," he repeated, though this time he spoke quietly, as if he felt some doubt.

"But what about you?" he asked, turning to Helena. "Why do you journey here, through the great Tundra Range? Few travellers arrive to hire a guide and mules, just to pass through the range. Most men are hunters—"

"I am not a man," she said.

"Tell me why you come."

"We're simply passing through."

"Going where? Up north? Nothing good lies up there. You do not look like Barberi."

"It's family business," said Helena quietly, staring across the hills as if to close him off.

"With the Barberi tribe? You are no friend to them. No one is friend to them. And what does that youth bear inside his shielding cloak?"

Helena spoke a prayer to brush thoughts from his mind. But, distracted as she was, she could tell by the big man's eyes that it had only partly worked.

When they made camp that night the air was cold enough for the party to put on furs. They made a small fire, then fed it with extra logs when the hunter's keen eyesight picked out a pack of wolves. Though they set a changing watch they found it hard to sleep when it was their turn to rest. The peaks oppressed them as they brooded overhead. The mules would not settle as they too sensed the wolves. It was a long, cold night, in which the only sounds were the crackling of the fire and an incessant monologue from a grumpy Pignikker, bemoaning everything.

But the small man from the swamp helped to lift the gloom somewhat by pointing out to them what a sorry bunch they were, and with the help of his flasks, which he had filled with ale, they somehow managed to get through the night.

CHAPTER 32

*B*y late next morning they were inside the mists circling the Tundra Range. Bulribar rode on to check the way ahead, while the others closed their line, which was straggling behind. They passed short silken ropes between the stiff saddles, and in this way bound the group. Grey wolves were following them, but still some way behind, and the hunter had set traps to slow down the leaders.

The Logra was also on their trail, but they had not spotted it yet, for it crouched within the rocks of a wind-ravaged spur. It seemed the beast of myth not only existed, but possessed intelligence.

A cold wind hit them as they emerged from the mists onto an icy path. They were above the snowline and thick flakes filled the air, sweeping down from the slopes to blind them. A mule reared up with shock and toppled from the path, plunging back through the mists. There was pandemonium before the silk rope snapped and the beast disappeared, leaving the rest behind. It seemed a bad omen so soon into the slopes, which now rose dizzily ahead.

They clung to a path of stone and ice, pressing against bare rock to keep out of the wind. Flakes swirled around their eyes and battered through their furs, chilling their exposed skin. The mules swayed as the wind tried to suck them off the path into the void. Pignikker let out a yell as his mule hit the rock, almost crushing his leg.

"Can't you make a spell, then? Are you a witch, or what?"

"I can't control this force – the elements are wild." Helena's voice was almost lost in the snorting of the mules and the howling of the wind.

Unable to advance at all, they sought a place to hide, and huddled dismally in a recess in the rock with the mules packed at their sides, thick furs draped on their backs and the ground a frozen mat. They tried to light a fire with kindling from the packs, but the wind blew out the flames and whipped away the wood. As they wrapped further scarves around their besieged mouths and eyes, ice crystals sought them out, lancing into the cave. Darkness came with the storm, touched by the ghostly grey of the snow-flakes on the wind.

"Is it always like this?" cried Pignikker, huddled at the rear.

"Sometimes," said Bulribar. "The blizzards come and go."

"I have a new respect for you. Working in a land like this would harden any man."

The mountain man grunted, and frowned uncertainly. "Is that a compliment?"

"It is the best I have."

"Well, you're okay yourself, for such a little man."

"Thanks," muttered Pignikker.

But that conversation was the only moment of cheer, for there was nothing the group could do to countermand the storm, and as the wind intensified they backed as far as they could into the dark recess. There was little warmth there and no comfort at all, and they felt a gloom descending over them. It was at that point, with their spirits at a low ebb, that the hungry mountain wolves launched their attack.

They came in snarling, in groups of three or four, bursting out of the gloom like hunting revenants. Ice-spikes clung to their fur, hunger blazed in their eyes, savagery gripped their jaws. As they propelled themselves towards the pack of mules, chaos entered the crowded space, and amidst a swirl of blood and the stench of canine fur, the band struggled to defend itself.

Helena checked Adam's arm as he went to draw his sword. "Leave it to the others," she said. "This fight is not for you." Adam stumbled back, knocked over by a wolf as the witch wielded a stick.

They fought with sticks and their bare hands, without the time to reach for a knife. They fought with tooth and nail, much as the wolves themselves fought.

Lina was howling with the blood-lust of the fight, and her mind seemed to flicker back to the wolves in the great forest. As she remembered the slaughtered deer, she pulled out a knife and fought. She slashed out savagely, ripping through matted fur. Four wolves fell at her feet and two more slunk from the cave. Her arm was torn but she did not heed the pain as she went to Pignikker's aid. The stocky man had fallen beneath a pack of wolves, and was struggling desperately to defend his throat and eyes. He was kicking with his heels, trying to force them off, when Lina joined the fray. The wolves were startled by the power of her approach, and Lina cut down two before they could regroup. Pignikker gained his feet, picked up a third wolf, and flung it from the cave.

But as suddenly as it had burst in, the wolf pack disappeared, leaving four slaughtered mules and two more bearing wounds. The cave rang with the sound of startled panting and barks, and the snow glistened with blood.

It was the witch Helena who noticed one man missing as she glanced around the cave at the bedlam the wolves had wrought. Her eyes were tense as they looked out at the raging storm. "Pignikker's gone," she said.

CHAPTER 33

"The wolves did not drag him off, and he did not go over the cliff," Bulribar said worriedly. "I was right here. I would have seen him fall. . . ." He peered down the plunging drop to the grey mists far below. "Pignikker did not fall. I swear on my own life I would have saved the man."

"He isn't here now, though," said the grey witch, trying desperately to conceal a rising dread.

"Something has happened to him—"

"*Well, that is obvious!*" the witch exploded. Then she took a long, deep breath. "I'm very sorry," she said. "Pignikker means a lot to me."

"He means a lot to me, too. He has become my friend. I am worried too," said Bulribar.

Once again the group searched for some sign of the former cattle thief, using the pale light of Raina's lantern to check the ground for footprints. There were fresh wolf tracks in abundance, fading even as they looked beneath new falls of snow, but there was no sign at all of the small man's thick-soled boots, nor any hint of injury. They spent a long time calling into the storm, receiving only the wind's laughter as a manic reply. The little man was gone, swept from the face of the earth as though he'd never been.

"He must be somewhere," muttered Helena, as she finally forced a brand to light. The dry twigs sputtered as she held aloft the torch, then poured out thick grey smoke like a swarm of silent wasps. It burned magnesium-white from the dust she threw on it from a small satchel. The flare made the mules jump, tense already following their brief affray with the half-starving wolves. They snorted in the gloom, their black hides glistening in the light cast by the brand.

Helena edged forward slowly, stepping over a pool of blood, holding the torch ahead to light the cavern's wall. Halfway along its length she saw a thin crack, as if the rock were hinged. She pressed against it and felt a draught of air, then turned to beckon Bulribar to come to her. "Push through the wall," she said.

"The wall?"

"It is not a wall, merely a screen of sorts set here by sorcery."

"I don't like sorcerers—"

"Push through the screen," she insisted, "if you seek Pignikker." The big man hesitated, studying the hairline crack, then pulled back his huge foot to slam it on the stone. There was an awesome crunch, and fragments of the wall fell like slaughtered bats. "Kick it again," she said.

Bulribar kicked out again and the whole long wall caved in, and through clouds of swirling dust the light from Helena's torch picked out a cave beyond. It was a vast place, big as a giant's tomb, where stalactites hung down like the teeth of dinosaurs. Long black pools drenched the floor, and in the first of them lay the fallen Pignikker.

"The little Pignikker!" Bulribar gave a cry and scrambled through the stones to reach his new-found friend. Helena was right behind, moving with surprising speed for someone of her years.

"He is such a warrior, this former carpenter. Did you see how he fought the wolves while lying on his back? That is unusual for such a little man. Must be a new technique."

Helena glanced at him, but Bulribar was sincere, filled with love for the former carpenter. His admiration knew no bounds, and his eyes were wet with tears as he gazed down on the man.

While the concerned pair knelt down to examine Pignikker, Adam and Lina fanned apart to explore the massive cave, creeping on silent feet, cautious of what might lurk in the ink-black dungeon depths. Adam sensed the Doom Sword thrumming against his back, but without the fire and heat that danger seemed to cause. It was as if the sword felt doubt, but not sufficient to bring alive its power. He did not draw it, remembering Helena's words, and the warning she had voiced without quite saying it – *Do not show Bulribar, and do not use the power.* They were getting close to their goal now. The Dark Lord must not know, and Bulribar might not be a good man to trust. So Adam kept the sword concealed, but felt exposed and vulnerable without its strong support.

Then the youth found a passageway at a corner of the cave, beyond the dripping piles which thrust down from the roof. A glow came from its depths: a sick, green graveyard light, as if cadavers burned. The smell which issued from the passageway was like incense which had blown through stinking fields, where maybe cows or dogs had lain in rotten piles. There was also a sense of threat and deep malevolence, of true depravity. . . .

CHAPTER 34

"It is a spell," said Helena after a time. "A sleep enchantment."

Lina was looking over her great-aunt's shoulder, watching her gently caress the carpenter's still face. "Can you not break the spell?"

"It is too deep for me. It is too powerful." Helena gave a sigh and glanced heavenwards, as if offering a prayer to her divinity. "It is so great a spell that even Pignikker, who is as strong as several bulls, may not recover from it. There is a road to lands where just the dead may go, and Pignikker walks it now. This is a foul deed, for he never harmed a man—"

"I will cut out his throat, the man that caused this!"

"I fear not, Bulribar. This is great sorcery – a master's handiwork." Helena's eyes glazed over as she remembered spells wrought in the past: spells which each bore the mark of the one who spoke the chants and wove the ancient arts. She had once studied under a great teacher called Lodrivar who had been offered banishment for preaching evil ways. She recalled his words, *"There is a fire in us which cannot be destroyed. But most men lose the flame, for it blows on the winds. We need to capture it. . . ."* This was what Helena had attempted with her own daughter's flame, forcing her to live inside a lamp which she could never leave. But maybe Lodrivar, the greatest of them all—

"The Logra fire . . ." she breathed.

They carried Pignikker along the freezing path towards the source of the glow.

It came from a green fire which blazed inside a cave whose walls sparkled with ice and whose floor was cold and bare. In the centre of the cave a hooded man sat on a rug, his face turned to the ground. He held a thin wand which twitched in his hands, as if he were conducting choirs no one else could hear. He had a long thin nose, and half the ear was missing from the left side of his face.

Bulribar held back as Helena checked his trembling arm from drawing out a knife.

"The witch Helena," a voice said quietly, though the man's lips never moved.

Helena answered. "That is my name," she said.

"And you do not know mine?"

"They called you Lodrivar."

"A long, long time ago." The man threw back his hood and turned his face to her. "The great mage Lodrivar, who you and all your kind drove into exile."

"We never drove you," the witch Helena said. "You volunteered for it."

Lodrivar gave a laugh. "The alternative was to be stripped of all my powers and left an empty shell of a man left stumbling round the world, performing party tricks, turning blood into wine. Oh yes, I 'volunteered'." His laugh was tolerant rather than bitter, as if he was resigned to things that might have been. "I could have been a king, master of all the arts—"

"But you chose demonry."

"Sit down, Helena, and your friends also. Their shuffling irritates me." Lodrivar shifted, as if to give them room, though the cave was large enough to hold a corps of troops.

"I would offer you a drink but the wine might

dull our minds, and we have much to talk about. You are carrying the Doom Sword—" Bulribar gave a start "—and hope to win the war against the poisoned king. And you may well succeed, for he is not so great as people think he is." He held up his hand, to pre-empt the group's response. "I do not want the Sword, for I crave something else. In return for the small man's life, and the lifting of the spell – I want Raina's soul."

"You cannot have her."

Lodrivar waved his hand, and Bulribar fell to the ground.

"Release your daughter's soul," he murmured patiently. "Or I'll kill all of them."

"And what will that gain you?"

"Nothing," said Lodrivar. "But they will all be dead." His dark eyes misted, as if they saw a place which few eyes ever saw or dreamed about. He said, "Have you ever looked into that awful pit which is eternity?"

Helena waited.

"It is a dreadful place, where nothing but the past can give you company. Such utter loneliness that it cannot be conceived – yet I have gazed on it. I have a place there, for it is my destiny; but I cannot go alone, for the bleakness torments me. I need Raina's soul to be my companion on that long journey."

"You shall not have her," Helena insisted, "though you kill all of us a thousand times or more."

"Easily done," he said. "And then I'll hand over the sword to Kalidor. The whole Kingdom, Helena, just for Raina's soul. Every little thing that breathes, every child, every maid, every man. Every mortal not yet born, every wish that's not been made. Every pain which is Kalidor's. . . ."

"You cannot do that," the witch said quietly. "It is too great a price."

"Nothing's too great a price when faced with endless lives spent in oblivion!" Lodrivar spat out his words with such ferocity that Adam and Lina flinched. "I will kill thirty worlds – a thousand – *every* world – to rescue my own fate."

"Which, if I remember, is why the Council members drove you from their ranks."

Lodrivar glared at Helena. "And you supported them. Think on it, Helena—" And, in an instant, the sorcerer was gone, leaving the rest behind trapped in a waiting spell. They heard his distant steps like hammers on the rock, then ringing emptiness . . .

"What do we do now?" Adam asked quietly, after some minutes had passed.

"Sit in the waiting spell. I can't fight Lodrivar,

he has too great a power. He taught us all he knew, and yet still held some back. He was the greatest of us all."

"Why doesn't he just take the soul?"

"She is bound up with my art, and dies without my power." Helena's eyes closed. "What a torment I have wrought by binding Raina's soul!"

They sat and waited for the sorcerer to return, listening to stalactites dripping down into the sick-green flames. They heard the mountain crack as the cold crept through its veins. They sensed the darkness wait. . . .

CHAPTER 35

"Have you decided?" said Lodrivar when he returned, dressed in a cloak of gold. He seemed much taller and more regal, his hair a flowing mane of glowing silver threads, as if he knew he'd win and had prepared himself for his trip into eternity. "There is no choice. You have to do my will, for I am Lodrivar."

"You are a black mage who should have been destroyed when we had you in chains."

"The price of mercy," the mage said pleasantly. "The price of giving in to what you call your soul, when you have no idea. *I* have a soul!" he cried. "I know what souls are for. I have a passion such as you will never know. For this, for life, I die, and offer up myself unto eternity!" He held his arms wide as if he were crucified, and his gaze turned heavenward as if to face his god. "I have such fire inside I would destroy this world—"

"You're mad," said Helena. But the witch was beaten, and she knew there was no choice, for she could not bear the name of the world's murderer. "You will destroy my child."

"I will make her a queen to rule oblivion."

Helena's face writhed with grief. "Let the child be," she breathed. "Show mercy on her soul."

"Where you showed none to mine? No, this is my triumph, my chance to beat the gods."

"The gods will punish you."

"I punish you," he hissed, "for being so naïve as to think you could banish me." Lodrivar's laughter went ringing through the flickering cave, a crescendo of tortured dreams and hopes – the sound of insanity. When it had faded the cavern seemed to rock, as if it was ill-prepared to cope with such a sound. The very stones themselves were stunned to hear such rage emerge from one man's lips.

"Give me the lamp!" he cried. "Hand her over to me!"

"I hope you rot in Hell," said Adam from the rear. And Raina's soul shook as Lodrivar plucked the flame from the lamp Helena held.

And in that instant, when Lodrivar's passion peaked, and for the briefest span he let his mind relax, Lina reached to her belt and took a hunting knife and hurled it at his heart. She flung it smoothly, but with all the strength she had, and it flashed through the air like a quick bolt of light. It passed straight through his chest and came out of his back, as if nothing was there.

"A cursed spectre!" Helena screamed with rage. "He has had me deceived, this was a *phandrigore!* Nothing but air and puff, and for this stupid trick I almost gave Raina's soul!" She swept up the flame and offered it to the lamp, but it paused upon her palm for maybe one heartbeat. And then it seemed resigned to its glass-sided fate, and slipped into its place.

Helena locked it in, then gathered up her skirts which had dropped in the pool which lined the cavern's floor. The sick-green flame was gone, Bulribar groaned on the ground, the enchantment was removed.

"Get Pignikker quickly, before Lodrivar comes, for he will now come himself, his spectre having failed. Blizzards and storms or not, we must press on with haste before he tracks us down."

Helena was already heading for the exit in the wall, muttering every prayer of defence that she had ever learned, and calling on ancient gods whose names were seldom heard to cover up their trail. . . .

Lodrivar caught up with them on a treacherous slope of ice and hard-packed snow. He was the *Logra*, a creature wrought of fire, which he'd formed with his will as a shield to encase his soul. He was a howling flame which swept down from the peaks like a blue avalanche.

Eagles came with him, as if to guard his flanks. Winds travelled in his wake, whipping up veils of snow. The group scattered from his charge, and only Adam stood to face the blaze and rage. He had uncovered the Doom Sword, disregarding Helena's words, and held it out in front in a two-handed grip. He had his feet well spread to give himself a base, and was staring intensely into the flame. His heart stopped in his chest as he waited for the fight. The only thing he knew was the rage which hurtled down the slopes at an ungodly pace.

The blue flame began screeching as the Doom Sword gave a hum, and became a tool of death dripping with black-tinged fire. Gone were its sparks and lights, gone was its angry blaze; this was a killing blade. Its every motion spoke of the death inside: a death which could cut souls and carve a slice from fire. This was the greatest force the world had ever known, and it filled

Adam's hands. It had waited centuries to meet such a foe as this: a foe without a form, a foe shaped of light. The darkness of the blade leapt out to meet the flame in a desperate conflict.

Adam was flung back as steam blasted his face. The Doom Sword seemed electrified with fright, as if the sword was stunned by the onslaught of the fire which contained Lodrivar's rage.

The flame was all around them, a swirl of heat and light in which there glowed a spark like an erupting heart. It was so pure and bright that it eclipsed the sky with its resplendence. It was like a diamond spitting out streams of light, streams which were so intense that they formed solid cords. And Adam hacked away the cords to reach the heart, which was the mage's soul.

He was fighting pure light, which was eating through his flesh. His limbs seemed to take fire and explode from his bones. But he was striding on, slicing through searing cords which screamed each time one died. The Doom Sword slashed and hewed and cut, tearing apart the threads and dimming the brilliant fire. But Lodrivar fought back, pouring out waves of light which shocked the universe.

They were killing Adam. They were reaching to his heart to rip out his soul. They were tearing through his mind and blotting out his thoughts.

Yet deep inside him a point of fire still burned, and he called on the fire and passed it to the sword, and as it flowed inside the sword rippled with light, and thrust into the soul.

It tore through Lodrivar, piercing him like a stake, hoisting him on its blade, tossing him like a rag. It ripped apart his soul and sent it to a void where nothing mortal lives. His scream was terrible, and deafened every ear. His pain was like the wind scouring the mountain's flank. His life was as the light which leaks around a door before it is slammed shut.

And Adam slammed it as fiercely as he could, so that the mountain shook and all men knew his name.

"I am the sword-bearer! Hear my name, Kalidor! I am the Lord of Death!"

Adam was shaking. Helena tenderly picked him up as if he were her child, shocked by a bad nightmare.

"It was the sword," she said. "And you are not the sword. You are its conqueror. . . ."

CHAPTER 36

The next day the travellers arrived at the Devil's Slide, the final obstacle on their journey through the bitter Tundra Range. It was a smooth sheet of silver glacial ice, almost a league in width and more than twice as high. It was so sheer and slick that even ibex hooves could not find a grip on it. When it plunged off a cliff it found a steep ravine, where rocks as sharp as knives waited to impale anyone who hurtled onto them. Of all the terrain within the Range, the Slide had wreaked most slaughter.

Wrapped in thick brown fox furs, Bulribar stared out across the trap, through dense clouds of his breath. "This is it, then. The final obstacle. The last threat we will face."

His friend Pignikker stood watching at his side, looking much like a boy standing beside a man. "How many times have you crossed it?" he murmured.

"This one will be my twelfth."

Behind them the rest of the group was tending the mules: making sure they were secure, throwing off excess packs, brushing and soothing the restless animals to reassure them. They were nailing spikes into the worn shoes on their hooves, brushing back their forelocks, checking that they could see. Nothing was overlooked in their desire to give the mules every chance possible.

It was a dry day, with clouds high in the air and a stiff breeze from the south scouring the slope. Small, distant dots were eagles in the sky, patrolling the peaks. Far below them they could see the swirling mists, and the brown foothills beyond, like islands on a sea. Cathedrals overhead were the spires of mountaintops, stretching towards their gods.

"This is as good a day as we shall ever find for crossing this terrain," Bulribar said, looking back. "Are you prepared?" he asked. "There is no time for doubt when we are on the slope."

The others nodded, checking again the rope

which linked them. Bulribar alone was not fastened to the rope, though he had it wrapped loosely around his left forearm. He feared that if he fell, his weight would pull the rest into oblivion.

"I'll take the lead," he said. "Pignikker comes behind. I cut our footholds, and you step into each one. If any mules should fall, just leave them to their fate. We cannot help them then." He raised his backpack and stared at Helena. "Will you not raise a spell to make our feet secure?"

"We have no need of spells," Helena said, "for we have Bulribar, the mountain warrior."

The big man grinned at her as he donned his massive pack, which bulged with clamps and spikes to drive into the slope. With a great axe in his hand, the towering mountain man stepped out onto the ice.

"Bulribar," said Pignikker, "have you ever been south to the lowlands?"

Bulribar grunted as he hammered in a massive spike, sweat streaming down his face, his eyes squinting against the light. They were halfway across, and gashes in the ice picked out their wandering course.

"I have – *oof!* – been as far as Drumdigar, but never further. I miss the mountains, I miss

the howling wolves, I miss this stupid slope."
He gave another swipe and stood up from the
spike, stretching his tiring back, cooling his
throbbing hands. "This is the life for me, though
I am not averse to making one more trip."

Pignikker nodded. "Come and stay with me,"
he said. "I know some seedy bars where you
would feel at home. I could show you my farm
and the cattle in my fields. I could show you my
barn."

"What's so good about a barn?" asked the big
man.

"I make my poteen there. It is a potent brew."

"I love your barn enough that I could die for
it," responded Bulribar. He gave a huge grin as
he slowly turned to scan the ice ahead, and the
route they should take. He shrugged his shrink-
ing pack into a better spot, and tucked away his
axe.

"I'll go up there now, and swing around this
bulge—" He pointed out the spot to which he'd
nail a spike. "You four stand as you are until the
rope's secure. This part is treacherous."

The others waited while the big man crept
ahead, his fingers in the snow, his toes digging
for grip. The cleats across his soles clutched at
the gleaming ice like cautious lizards' feet. He
advanced slowly, trusting nothing at all except
his own strong hands and the probings of his

feet, and he was caught unawares when they both let him down, and he slipped. There was a moment when Bulribar's fingers almost gripped, then he began to slide down the unyielding slope. He tried to reach his axe but it caught in his belt.

"I'm going, Pignikker—" Bulribar said the words with a desperate calmness, and the look on his face was one of disbelief, for the slope was sliding past faster than he could grip – faster than he could think.

There was a sudden, strangled cry from the startled Pignikker, as he flung himself full length to save his falling friend. He grabbed him by the wrist and was carried down the sheer slope after him. The others braced themselves against the coming shock, clutching at the sliding rope as if it held their lives. As the weight of two grown men slammed on their straining arms, they crumbled at the knees.

"*I have you, Bulribar!*" shouted the little man. "*I have you by the hand, and shall not let you fall!*" But every muscle screamed inside Pignikker's arms, and every sinew roared. The pressure on his clutching hand mounted remorselessly; he bit down with his teeth until his lips poured blood. Stars flashed inside his eyes as he clung to his friend and gazed into his eyes. "I shan't release you—"

"I'm going, Pignikker—" Bulribar knew this fact as clear as any truth. As he watched Pignikker's eyes and saw his desperate pain, he felt his body lurch. "You would have made a good friend. *We* would have made good friends—" And with a sudden cry the mountain man was gone, slipping backwards down the ice, beyond all hope of help, as Pignikker yelled at him.

They watched each other all the way through the drop, until Bulribar was just a dot plunging across the ice; and as he vanished from the edge into the fall beyond, they heard a lonely cry.

For a long time the group could not move or speak, but remained staring at the spot where Bulribar had been. The white eagles overhead slowly increased in size, as if drawn by the screams.

"We cannot stay here," said Helena, as the group stood helplessly upon the hostile ice. All the spikes were gone and the riving axe was lost. They could not take a step without following Bulribar, and the eagles were closing in and storm clouds were threatening. "We have to do something. Use the Doom Sword, Adam, to take us out of here."

Adam's eyes stared at the witch as if she were a stranger, numbed by the loss of the man who had been their guide and friend.

"Use the Doom Sword," Helena repeated. "Ignore dark Kalidor. We need protection now."

Adam nodded distractedly, as if lost in a dream, and glanced around the slopes as if searching for something. "What about Bulribar?"

"The man is gone from us into another place, and we cannot help him now." Helena stared hard at him, trying to draw him back, slipping spells into him to make him strong again. He seemed to hesitate, then came back to himself as veils slid from his eyes.

"We must go on then, or it will be a pointless death, and all that we've achieved will be as dead as him. We must go on to fight and defeat Kalidor, or darkness will prevail."

Helena nodded, and moved to let Adam pass as he reached for his pack to take out the Doom Sword. "I hoped to save its power to fight dark Kalidor—"

"Now is its time," she said.

So Adam strode ahead of the group, hacking a narrow path, blazing with fire and light and panting out grey breath. And as the clouds came down, bringing a dim twilight, he led them off the ice.

CHAPTER 37

The rushing Zinniga Ford was not such an obstacle after all they'd been through. They sent a mule through to draw away the zander-shark, having put spells on it so that it would feel no pain, and as its body slid downstream they splashed across the ford into Barberi land.

The landscape was open and desolate, a place of rounded rocks all uniformly grey. It was no place to farm or set a thriving town, so the Barberi moved on constantly. They raised their reed hut homes, pulled them down again and packed them onto carts, moving from the coast-line in the north where they killed whales and seals, to the bears' home in the east. They pillaged travellers who journeyed through their land, for they were wild and fierce and jealous of their home. But now they were far away, hunting a pack of seals drifting down the coast.

A day of riding brought the group to Parter's Leap, a jagged spur of land which overlooked a gorge. In the distant west, framed by the setting sun, they saw the Bridge of Doom. It was a grey arch not seven metres deep, stretching across a void some forty metres wide. The void was called Oblivion. Nothing could live there, none could survive there; all who fell in the mists were simply swept away. No one but Adam knew what lay beyond the void. None lived to tell the tale.

As he reined in Alon and watched the setting sun, he thought this a fit time for his strange flight to end, for the Kingdom mapped below, silent and full of fear, seemed to be watching him.

"Do we go down now?" he asked.

"Rest now," Helena said. "We will descend at dawn with sunlight at our backs. Tonight we try to sleep, for in the coming dawn, the Lord of Darkness waits."

Kalidor waited with four of his finest swordsmen beside him. He had no sorcerers, for he had no use for them now, nor would he trust his hordes close to the Doom Sword. So the men that he had picked were his most loyal slaves, with no will of their own.

He watched the group approach, picking its cautious way down a steep, rocky path which wound towards the gorge. They had set free the mules, for this was not their fight and they had served their part.

A burst of lightning flickered above his head. A peal of thunder crashed as he took out his sword and strode to meet the group halfway towards the Bridge.

He spoke first to Adam. "Lay down your arms."

The witch replied. "Step from our path," she said, "for your dark reign is done."

Kalidor tossed back his head and laughed, and the darkness of his throat echoed oblivion. He wore a cloak of unrelenting black and a helm of polished steel, and carried a shield of fire and brass. "Defy me, witch," he said, "and you shall roast in flames for all eternity!"

Adam drew the Doom Sword, and said, "Move from the path."

But still the Dark Lord laughed, secure within his power. He said, "I have put out the light of the Eternal Fire, and your quest is over."

Helena staggered visibly at the words. "You cannot quench the Fire!" she said. "The flame can never die!"

"It was no easy task," the Lord of Night replied. "It cost me sorcerers." He gestured backwards, across the windswept gorge, to where the Fire Pit lay in a depression in the rocks. The flame had always blazed – men said it always would – but now the Pit was empty.

Helena's senses swam as she saw the end of her hopes of freeing the Doom Sword. Without the endless Fire the sword would rage and grow through all eternity.

"You cannot do that," she whispered, her shattered hopes and dreams leaving her withered and grey. "The Fire must never die—"

The Dark Lord's laughter rang out, over Oblivion. . . .

CHAPTER 38

The figure of the Ancient Warrior sped across the plain which fronted the Bridge of Doom. He was mounted on a beast of Dornok, which rode on silver wings and turned the plain to ash as fire dripped from its hooves. The reiver Robart tried in vain to match the pace on his own black steed, but he was falling further and further to the rear as the demon warrior sensed the nearness of the sword.

The Warrior's eyes were full of pain and his mind full of hate as he closed on the blade. Nothing could stop him, for he brought the power of Hell. Nothing could cut him down, for he possessed no soul. All he brought was rage, which had waited a thousand years for just this time.

"My lord—!" cried Robart, but the demon did not hear, for he was nearing his blade. . . .

"Put down the sword," the Dark Lord murmured uneasily.

Adam was approaching, the sword stiff in his hands. His eyes were blazing pools of darkness touched with fire. His muscles were so taut that the shirt across his back seemed to be rippling.

The Dark Lord backed off, driven towards the Bridge, his own sword hanging loose as if it feared to fight. But deep within his eyes a spark of evil burned, waiting its time to strike.

"The Ancient Warrior!" a man screamed from the Bridge, as he saw the soulless demon cross the blazing plain. The thunder of hooves drowned out all thought and sound, and made the dark sky writhe.

"It is the demon!"

"Silence, mindless fool!" Kalidor did not look round. He did not take his gaze from the grim Doom Sword. His heart was beating fast, his lips were thin and taut. "Give me the sword," he breathed.

"Go back to your dark isle!" Adam said as he sprang to strike, swinging the sword aloft and sweeping it through an arc. There was a flash of light and a clash of ringing blades as the Lord's sword met the blow.

"Pignikker! The swordsmen!" the witch Helena cried, and the stocky man ran forward, swinging a woodsman's axe. Charging onto the Bridge, he laid into the men with startling fury.

As they retreated and the Dark Lord fought Adam, Lina dropped to the ground and raised her long crossbow. With her arm braced on one knee, her bow covered the plain, seeking the demon. She could not stop him, but she could kill his horse and bring down the demon to buy them precious time. Sweat trickled down her face as she watched the great horse dripping its rain of fire.

The battle raged back onto the Bridge of Doom as Adam continued to advance. Time and again he struck with the full force of his blade, driving back the Dark Lord, beating him to the ground; and time and again the Dark Lord rose and turned away the blows. Lightning flashed across the Bridge and the thunder of their swords made the whole landscape shake. The battle could be heard throughout the land, even to Paridoor.

Dark clouds were closing in as the Warrior thundered on, his horse a blaze of fire, his black sword in his hand, while Lina crouched and shook, praying for one clean shot. For his horse was shifting, as if it flowed in waves, and Lina could not find a spot at which to aim. As the horse leapt down on her she closed her eyes and fired, and the arrow pierced its chest.

The beast of Dornok crashed inside a rage of fire and rocks torn from the earth. It died like a phoenix returning to its grave, with wings of silver flame and lightning in its heart. It died like all the fires of a volcanic range erupting in one burst.

But even in its death throes the horse had a part to play, for the Dark Lord snatched its soul and forged it with his own, calling on all the powers of darkness and the night to aid him in his fight. Blazing with madness, he struck as Adam tired, driving home massive blows which would have split a god. He forced him off the Bridge and back onto the rocks.

Still Kalidor strode ahead, pounding with all his strength, using his mighty sword like a great battle-axe. As Adam's strength gave out beneath the sustained onslaught, Kalidor snatched the sword from him. . . .

CHAPTER 39

Kalidor the Master, the Prince of the Universe, brandished the glowing blade of the ecstatic sword in the face of God. He taunted heaven, sending flames from its tip to penetrate the clouds and flood the sky with light. He built a massive storm which raged about his head and tore his tattered cloak.

He flung up fury as if to banish God, and darkness spread about him like a veil of night. Death lived inside his heart, and now he had the power to fling it through the world. When he laughed, volcanoes split the world; when he let out a cry, great oceans burst their shores. When he brought down his hand a chasm ripped the land, as the Doom Sword touched the earth.

This was his moment, his hour of destiny: a time when all the world bent down to kiss his hand . . . except for one small form, crawling across the rocks; the grey witch Helena. As darkness poured down and thunder filled the air, the brave witch clawed her way towards her daughter's soul, beaten on by the storm, lashed by the torrential rain pouring out of the sky.

She reached the lantern and pulled back its cover, watching her daughter's flame flickering valiantly. "Relight the Fire and drive darkness away," she begged. "Try to forgive me. . . ."

The Ancient Warrior, thrown from his slaughtered horse, dragged himself to his knees and looked round for his sword. And when he saw Kalidor blind hatred filled his thoughts with the wrath of demons.

But Kalidor raged on oblivious to all this, drinking the rain of God as if it were his wine. His dark face mocked the sky, his bare throat was exposed . . . and Pignikker sprang at him. He put his knife to Kalidor's throat, but the Dark Lord gripped him by the hand, then bent back his whole arm until the shoulder snapped. The small man gave a cry and Kalidor flung him, spiralling, into the void. Helena's voice shrieked out as she saw her true love fall. She dropped the open lamp and ran towards the gorge, calling Pignikker's name.

The Ancient Warrior stumbled onto the Bridge, still wounded from his fall and clutching at his side. He drew his own black sword and, swaying painfully, limped to meet Kalidor. And in that instant the soul of Raina emerged from her lamp like a bird made of flame. She flew to Adam's side and said, "*You are my love . . .*" Then she was gone, streaking upwards beyond the Bridge of Doom into a jet-black sky where she shone like a star. And she paused for one brief look before she hurtled down into the Pit of Fire.

The Pit erupted in a great ball of light, and in its raging heart Raina's form shone briefly. Adam saw the girl she was, saw the youthful beauty of her face – and then she vanished. The wind took hold of her and spread her like a mist, leaving only her words to whisper in his brain. The last thing Raina said before she disappeared was, "*You are my desire. . . .*"

As Kalidor looked round, shocked by the rush of flame, the Warrior reached out to grab him by the hand. The Doom Sword fell to the ground as the pair became entwined in a desperate combat.

Adam stared at the sword, afraid to pick it

up, afraid to make a move for his body hurt so much. But he heard Lina's voice saying, "For all your life you have been trained for this. Your grandfather trained you—" He turned to look at her. She was lying on her side, nursing a brutal wound from the fallen Dornok horse. As she looked into his eyes, her face writhing with pain, she said, "Take up the sword. This is the hour for you. We need you, Adam . . ."

Adam started crawling, hauling his battered limbs, creeping one step at a time towards the Bridge of Doom. His eyes were locked on the sword, his pain locked in his teeth, breath snorted out of him. As his hand closed around the hilt he felt his body thrill, and the Doom Sword's rage and power came rushing back to him. And he struggled to his knees, then rose to his feet and held aloft the sword. . . .

But the Ancient Warrior and the Dark Lord rushed at him, and Adam was thrown back by the force of their advance. As all three gripped the sword the Bridge of Doom collapsed, and they plunged into the void. Adam started screaming as he hurtled through the mist, sensing that Kalidor was reaching out to him.

But the Dark Lord disappeared, swept off on different tides, finding his own grim fate. And it seemed there was nothing but falling, and a sense of endless time – a time touched by a flame which runs through all mankind. The very flame of life which keeps each soul alight, braving the Doom Sword. . . .

CHAPTER 40

He woke up gradually in the small bedroom where he had first picked up the sword. Shadows were falling across the empty bed. Noises came from downstairs as his parents returned home. He felt the leaden weight of the sword clutched in his hand – the once mighty Doom Sword.

But it was not flickering, nor did it pulse with power. It did not give out light nor set his soul on fire. It was only a sword, rusting and slightly scarred from the uses it had known.

He sat up slowly, rubbing his aching arms, and watched the fading dreams go drifting from his mind. The last thing he saw was the grey witch Helena, descending through the gorge. She was trying to climb down to rescue Pignikker, her skirt tucked in her belt and her clutching fingers raw. He thought of Lina's face, and the last look she wore. He saw Raina's soul. But these things were fading like ripples on a pond, drifting back into time as if they had never been, until there was nothing but the sound of Raina's voice whispering inside his brain, *"Behold, the sword-bearer. . . ."*

Peter Beere

Peter Beere lives in Lancaster with his wife, Marty and his pet dog. Together they run the Lancaster Night Shelter for the Homeless. Peter's interest in homeless people began when he lived in London, where he would often see people huddled in doorways. What shocked him most was he recalls, not "that there were so many of them, but that so many of them were so *young*."

It was around this time that he began to work on *Crossfire*, his first novel for teenagers (he had previously published several books for adults), which deals with the plight of Maggie, a young runaway. His next work, the *Underworld* trilogy is written both as a series of exciting adventure stories, but also as a warning that life on the streets is very hard and often dangerous.

Peter says that he writes the kinds of stories that he would like to have read when he was a teenager. He has recently published *School for Death* in Scholastic's Point Crime series, and is planning another crime story, *Kiss of Death* for next year. He is currently writing *Riot*, also to come out next year.

Look out for this exciting fantasy adventure also available in Point Fantasy:

BROG THE STOOP

Joe Boyle

Brog was swept along with the mass of bodies, each trying desperately to keep out of reach of the savage enemy.

In the crush, he lost sight of Blid, and of Plin and Pik, and he fought to catch sight of them in the crowd.

He was able to catch only glimpses of what was happening as he was carried along.

In the few minutes since the attack had begun, the Stoop had suffered heavy losses, and bodies seemed to be strewn everywhere. Klan and his warriors could be seen fighting valiantly in a number of places, supported by bands of plain Stoop, swords flashing, making full use of their superior speed of foot, and more than one Gork fell screaming.

Brog felt so utterly helpless, and wished with all his heart that he could be fighting like them instead of merely struggling to keep upright in the surge of fleeing bodies.

One Gork stood out amongst the rest.

He was half as big again as any of the others, and seemed to be directing operations from a point in the centre of the Flatplace, but the single feature which really separated him from his murderous counterparts was his eyes, and Brog's blood ran cold as he saw them.

The eyes of this giant Gork were pure evil, piercing, and a bright, glowing red!

As the Stoop reached the trees, the crowd thinned, and Brog found he had time to stand and look around for familiar faces.

Klan and his band were fighting a brave, but losing battle, and were being driven nearer and nearer to the trees at the far side of the clearing. It was obvious that, in a matter of minutes, they too would be forced to break off and retreat, though the time they had bought by their brave actions had been invaluable.

Brog scanned the passing faces, searching for some hope that Blid and the others had escaped the dreadful slaughter, but nowhere could he see those he had lost.

"Brog! Brog!" A shout to his right.

It was Pik, and he was beckoning furiously from the fringe of the trees.

In the centre of the Flatplace, Redeye turned his head as he heard the voice, and saw the tall, young Stoopling run across, making for the fringe.

His Gork had done well, many Stoop lay dead, the Stoopwarriors were being driven to retreat.

A little killing of his own would be quite pleasant.

Turning, he lumbered in pursuit of the Stoopling, fangs bared in a snarl.

From the corner of his eye, Brog saw Redeye moving to the attack, and he put in a burst of speed. Redeye gave a roar, fearing that his victim was about to escape him, and changed the angle of his charge in an effort to cut him off.

"Faster, Brog, faster!" urged Pik.

Brog's long legs were covering the ground at a tremendous pace, and it was touch and go whether he reached the trees before, or at the same time as Redeye.

A figure hurtled past Brog from out of the bushes, too fast for him to see who it was, but he heard the roar of surprise from Redeye, and the thud of bodies behind him before he was grabbed by Pik, and dragged, still running, into the thickness of the Treelands.

Redeye tore viciously at the Stoopmother who had prevented him from catching the speeding young one and, knowing that she had made Brog's escape possible, Blid died.

POINT HORROR
Read if you dare. . . .

Are you hooked on horror? Are you thrilled by fear? Then these are the books for you. A powerful series of horror fiction designed to keep you quaking in your shoes.

Mother's Helper
by A. Bates

April Fools
The Lifeguard
Teacher's Pet
Trick or Treat
by Richie Tankersley Cusick

My Secret Admirer
by Carol Ellis

Funhouse
The Accident
The Invitation
The Window
The Fever
The Train
by Diane Hoh

Thirteen
by Christopher Pike, R.L. Stine and others

Beach Party
The Baby-sitter
The Baby-sitter II
The Boyfriend
The Snowman
The Girlfriend
Hit and Run